Cap

D0814437

Vikings

Captured by the Vikings

Torill Thorstad Hauger

translated by
Marlys Wick Paulsen

Breakwater
100 Water Street
P.O. Box 2188
St. John's, Newfoundland
A1C 6E6.

Published with grants from the Norwegian Cultural Council and Nordmanns-Forbunder (The Norsemen's Federation), Oslo.

Canadian Cataloguing in Publication Data
Hauger, Torill Thorstad, 1943-
      Captured by the Vikings
      Translated from Norwegian.
      ISBN 1-55081-033-2
I. Title.
PZ7.H38Ca 1991 j839.8'2374 C91-097549-3

*The events of this story
are set in the tenth century.*

Part I

*R*eim awoke with a start. Fright shuddered through his body. His hands searched frantically along the cold, stone wall until he found the opening and pulled out the rag that darkened the hole. The cold air hit his face. Outside, he caught a glimpse of silver grey trees with branches grasping towards the moon, stretching high up into the heavens.

So, it was not just a bad dream after all. He really was in this frozen land so far north, with a new, long winter on the doorstep. It was as if nature was waiting for the first snowflakes to whirl over the land and change the world into a stiff, white landscape.

Reim covered the opening and spied into the dark room. He caught a glimpse of Digralde, leaning against the wall, listening intensely to the night. And suddenly he remembered, remembered why he had slept so uneasily this night. This was the night it had to happen. This was the night that they had to escape. That was why Digralde now kept watch.

Reim laid down in the hay again and curled tightly into his sister. Her back was so warm and comforting, reminding him of everything that he had loved. It felt as if a whole lifetime had passed since he was seized from his home in Ireland. And when he closed his eyes, he could picture his father's protective, earth-soiled hands, his mother's vigilant gaze, and the wrinkled, aged face of his grandmother Gaelion, as she sat rocking back and forth, telling strange tales and legends.

The summer was finer that year than he could remember it ever having been. He could understand why they called Ireland the greenest of all islands in the whole world. The grass was so thick and green that it was nearly luminous, and daisies filled the fields. The heavens were high and wide and filled with sunshine. Yes, he even remembered that their dappled cow bore twin calves that summer, and on the neighbouring farm, that family's tenth child came into the world.

His name was Patric then. A good old Irish name. Once, when he was quite little, he had asked his mother why he had that name. She had laughed and taken him upon her lap. "We named you after someone who lived in Ireland a long, long time ago," she said. "His name was also Patric. Legend says that he was captured by a foreign people, and that he was a slave for many years before he was finally set free. Patric was a pious man who was made holy after his death. Now Saint Patric is regarded as the greatest saint in all of Ireland."

Her green eyes glittered jokingly as she continued. "Old people say that children usually acquire the same qualities as the person they are named after. But I can't quite believe that you will ever be a saint, my dear little pirate!" And she pinched him lovingly on the cheek.

No, his mother had been right there. He would never be a saint. As often as he could, he tried to get out of working there: on the farm. He slipped quickly over secret paths into the forest and hid in the tops of old, knotted oak trees. He raced with the horses in the pasture and rolled over and over in the high grass that smelled of summer and sun.

When his father caught him, he pulled him up by the hair and said, "There had better be an end to the likes of this tumbling around of yours." His eyebrows drew together like dark thunder clouds. "Why, you resemble a grasshopper, dancing and singing the whole summer through, you do! But you know that after summer comes autumn, for us all. I certainly don't know what kind of a farmer you are ever going to make, you little scamp!"

Patric knew enough to be ashamed. What his father said was true. If anyone asked him to milk a cow, he thought, laughing a bit to himself, he would probably begin by pumping it's tail.

Their farm was on the edge of a village, close to the walls of a monastery. He could clearly see the three small stone houses with their thatched roofs and the lavish grazing lands that stretched down to the sea, where their dappled cow and four ragged goats grazed.

Disturbances in Ireland were common. Great men and warriors fought constantly for land and riches. Sometimes they heard of groups of robbers from other lands that ravaged the coastlines of Ireland. "But here, thank goodness, we live quite safely," his mother sighed as they gathered around the table during the evening. "This is a blessedly quiet and peaceful corner of God's earth...."

But Grandmother Gaelion laughed so her round belly shook. "Quiet and peaceful, you say! For my part there certainly is enough fighting and disturbances in this house every single day, and that includes the holy days. With five wild children here on the farm, there is never much peace and quiet!"

Some of the things that happened that summer he remembers better than others. Like the time he and Brian managed to secure a dinner that the whole district would have envied them—if they had known about it.

Brian was the second oldest boy on the neighbouring farm. As long as Patric could remember, he and Brian had been like two intertwined weeds. When they were small, they competed against each other; who was the strongest, who could hang the most worms on their belt, and who could send the longest jet streaming right over the roof of the sheep barn. He laughed when he thought of that last feat because he drank buckets of water to achieve it and practised diligently every day.

But then they outgrew those childish games and instead made bows out of supple willow branches. They pretended that they were the royal archers that lived in a huge, enchanted forest. They explored the forest and found paths that no one else knew of, and they captured the bandits that sat hidden high up in the towering oaks. Swish! The arrows flew to the top of the trees and whistled through the forest.

Patric fought constantly with his sister, Sunniva, that summer, as she insisted on tagging after him and wanted to be wherever anything exciting was going on. To begin with they let her join in their games. They always needed someone to tie up the thieves as they fell out of the trees. But one day she took a bow and showed them that their helper was a steadier shot than the royal archers themselves. This irritated Patric to no end. He made a law proclaiming that all archers had to be men.

One day as they sneaked through the forest on moss-lined paths, Brian stopped and took Patric's arm. Wasn't there something over there in the leaves? They stood dead still, not a muscle moved.... Yes, there in the thicket. A large, red-brown animal. The sun shone down on its smooth skin.

Noiselessly, they drew their bows. Patric wasn't sure who shot first, but suddenly an arrow whistled in the wind. The animal jumped out of the thicket, and fell lifelessly on the ground.

Brian reached it in one jump. "A deer!" he screamed, his voice hoarse in excitement. "Royal archer, we have shot a deer!"

Patric stood petrified and stared at the animal. He didn't like seeing one of the forest's proud animals lying lifeless on the ground. But he didn't have time to think much about it. Brian threw himself around Patric's neck, and they hopped and danced and laughed around and around each other.

How long they toiled to get that heavy animal home with them, heaven only knows. They took off their belts and tied the animal by its fore and back feet to a solid pole. Then they lifted the pole to their shoulders and dragged it, step by step, home. By the time they reached the farm the Great Bear was already high in the dark sky, blinking at them over the roof of the sheep barn.

Father met them out in the yard. In the clear evening air, they could see his astonishment and fright. "In the name of Saint Patric, boys, what have you done now?"

"Can't you see that we have shot a deer, father!"

"Anyone with eyes in his head can see that. I think you are both out of your minds. If the owner of these forests finds out about this, we all are in trouble. Not long ago a poacher was caught, and he hangs and dangles from the end of a rope even now!"

"No one saw us," Brian said calmly. "We shot it on one our secret paths."

"Oh, Saint Patric be praised! We will just have to hope for the best then." His father's face ironed out again. "You, run home and get help, Brian. We can divide the spoils." Suddenly he smiled and licked his lips. "It is just too seldom that a small farmer gets a taste of venison!"

That evening was like Christmas Eve in the middle of June. The delicious smell of venison steak swirled throughout the room. There on the long bench sat Mother, Father and Grandmother Gaelion, their faces blissful, their stomachs full of tender deer meat. The stone slab in front of the hearth was tightly packed with five small brothers and sisters. They sighed happily. The five heads of hair shone like bronze in the light from the crackling fire. Patric smiled as he thought of what a neighbour lady used to say about them. "When all five of you Neal children are here, if is almost as if I have a great fire right in the middle of my hut." Patric knew very well what she meant. They got their red hair from their father. He didn't have many hairs left on his head now, but his beard was as red as an oak tree in full autumn dress.

When they were finished with their meal, his father stood up rather laboriously and patted his stomach. He walked over and rustled Patric's hair, and then said something that nearly made Patric burst with pride. "Perhaps one day you will make a good farmer after all, you scamp."

About the time of the year when the strawberry fields cast a red glow over the hillsides, Brother Cormac waddled across the yard.

"I bet that he has come to taste some of our good plum wine again this year," Sunniva said and giggled. They could not keep track of all of the times Brother Cormac had found some kind of excuse to come and wet his whistle in the company of good neighbours. But this time it seemed that he had other things on his mind. His round, good-natured face fairly vibrated with this suppressed secret. He asked Neal to follow him out to the pasture.

"What in the world is this all about?" Father wondered, smiling and scratching his beard. He swung his axe into the chopping block and followed the friar across the field. The children flew after them, hopping up and down like curious rabbits in the tall grass.

They walked past the tall bell tower and along the endless walls of the monastery. They bowed under the weeping willows down by the river and crawled through the willow brush where hundreds of small sparrows sat, singing in the evening sun. When they finally reached the pasture, Brother Cormac opened the gate in the stone fence and pointed. Right in the middle of the field stood a light grey colt. She lifted her head and stared with bright, frightened eyes at the two-legged creatures that were approaching. The colt looked as if she would dart away at any moment. But Brother Cormac quickly tempted her with a whole fist-full of sweet clover. "Come now, Stella. Come now...."

The colt could not resist clover. She darted across the field on her thin, unsteady legs, snapping after the clover and cocking her head trustfully towards them.

"What a beautiful animal," their father said.

"Yes, and now it is *your* colt," Brother Cormac replied. He cleared his throat and made himself quite brisk. "We brothers at the monastery are quite tired of you borrowing our horses all of the time."

Their father smiled broadly under his untidy beard. His face looked exactly as it used to on holidays, as he patted the colt's neck. "No, this gift is just too precious, brother Cormac. I have always wanted to own a horse."

"Yes, well. It is just a return for the help you gave us in building the new roof on the monastery church!" Brother Cormac winked teasingly as he saw the five children sneaking up to pat the horse. "You have quite a flock of frisk colts here, I see. Can't be easy to tame a flock like this!"

He tugged their hair lovingly and laughed the loud rumbling laugh they all knew so well. His stomach rolled back and forth under his brown monk's robe.

Father gave Patric the reins and let him lead the colt towards their farm. Patric leered smugly at Sunniva. She was one year younger, and she was just a girl. She could take care of the calves and their dappled cow. But as if reading Patric's thoughts, their father suddenly stopped and said, "Little Sunniva will take care of this colt. She has such a good way with animals."

Sunniva's mouth rippled into a triumphant smile, and she danced so her long braids twirled around her head. "Mother," she called when she saw her mother's brown smock over by the barn, "come see our new colt!"

"Her name is Stella," lisped their little brother, Roderic. "Brother Cormac says that it is Latin and means star. Can you see that she has a big, white star on her forehead?"

Mother set the buckets she was carrying down on the ground and came to meet them. Fine, laugh lines fanned out from her beautiful eyes, which were the same emerald green colour as the rest of the island. She clapped her hands. "What a beautiful little colt!" And then she adjusted her shawl as she hesitantly asked if Brother Cormac would do them the honour of coming into their humble home and join them in a glass of plum wine. Well, now, he really didn't have time for that, the monk said, but this was a special occasion, so....

They sat on the bench that was fastened to the wall under the little window, and the evening sun reflected on the polished head of the monk and on the bronze-coloured beard of the farmer. Father talked at great length about so many things, lightly, like a spring creek bubbling over. "This has truly been a good summer," he laughed. "It is as if we have been blessed by two suns in the heavens the whole summer through. Lift your glass, Brother Cormac!"

Grandmother Gaelion smiled at the two men sitting there on the bench. She sat bowed over her spinning wheel, taking advantage of the last rays of daylight to spin yarn from the brown sheep's wool. Mother came in with two wooden buckets. They smelled of sweet, warm milk. She ladled the milk into bowls and gave them each a piece of bread. And then she said, as she always did, "Thank God, dear children, that we can go to bed on full stomachs...."

How strange that the grown-ups could be so serious on such a fine summer evening. "Yes, we have much to be grateful for," their father said. He sat staring at his enormous, soiled hands. "It is a farmer's duty to take care of the land. But a free farmer is his own master. That is a great thing, it really is...."

And then he lifted his glass and emptied it as Brother Cormac emptied his.

Only those boys who were to be priests, or who were the sons of rich, great men were allowed to attend the monastery school. But Brother Cormac said that since Patric nearly pestered him to death with his questions, he could find a place to sit in the back of the classroom. There he sat and fought with his feather pen and ink and a stiff skin from an old cow. Brother Cormac would not give him a calf skin to start with.

Patric dipped the feather pen into the ink well and scratched across the cow skin. "No, no boy, not like that," said Brother Cormac as he pulled at his little wreath of grey hair. "You have to paint the letters! Paint them carefully, beautifully, I say!"

Patric threw himself into this work, his tongue tip protruding from the corner of his mouth, and he did not give up until he had learned the correct symbols. When he came home that evening he tried to show Sunniva and Grandmother Gaelion the art of writing. Grandmother Gaelion smiled and shook her head. "Terrible what they have figured out there at the monastery to pass the time of day...."

It was at the monastery that Patric heard, for the first time, of the dangers threatening Ireland's people.

One day, after all of the other boys had gone, Patric sneaked as quickly as a chipmunk over to niche in the wall and took out one of the huge, fine leather-bound books that he did not have permission to touch. He opened the book, and his eyes grew wide in amazement, for the pages were painted in such fine, clear colours that it was as if the angels themselves had done them. The largest letters glittered in the purest gold, and between them twined dragons and fantasy animals. Here and there, small pictures of the saints peeked out at him, so real that it looked as if they would jump right out of the book and start talking to him.

Then he heard a voice in the monastery garden. A foreign man stood talking to Brother Cormac. His voice was loud and excited. "I say that I saw it with my own eyes. The whole town is burned down. The monastery has been ravaged, and many of the monks are dead. The devil's men themselves have been on a raid. The vikings!" And then he told of such horrible happenings that Patric felt fear creeping down his back.

When the foreign monk had gone, he ran over to Brother Cormac who stood hoeing his vegetable garden. He clung to the rope tied around the thick stomach of the monk. "Is it true, Brother Cormac? Is what the foreign monk told true? About the horrible warriors from the north...."

"Calm down now, boy. You are squeezing the air out of me. If you had gone home in due time, you would not have heard things that are not meant for your ears. Now, stop trembling, boy. There is no reason to have nightmares right in the light of day. What this monk told of happened many a day's travel from here."

Brother Cormac set his hoe aside and took Patric by the shoulder. "You don't think that anything like that can happen here, in this peaceful little corner of God's earth?"

No, of course he couldn't believe that. But that summer rumours spread like fire in dry grass through the little country village.

"Vikings," mother said. "Yes, of course, I have heard of the vikings. They have ravaged our country for years, but I refuse to tell tales of such warriors just before bedtime." She held out a bowl of warm goat's milk. "Drink this," she said. "Warm milk gives sweet dreams." And then she closed the door as she went outside.

"I wonder if she is just going to the barn or all the way out in the pasture to fetch Stella," Roderic whispered. As soon as his mother was out of the door, he placed a naked foot down on the earth floor and flew across the room, over to the bench bed near the hearth. "Grandmother," he whispered and shook the skin rug. "Grandmother, are you sleeping?"

"Yes, as a matter of fact, I was," Grandmother grunted. Her long, grey braids were barely visible over the edge of the skin rug. "Just now I was fast asleep and no one was bothering me. There wasn't even anyone begging me to tell a pirate story."

But then she turned to Roderic and winked at him teasingly. "Well, you can all come then."

Soon they all sat together under her huge skin rug. Grandmother laboriously pulled herself up and leaned against the bench post. Her face was like a wrinkled, aged winter apple, but her eyes glittered brightly. They resembled small, glassy water holes, where tales and legends swirled way down in the deep. Grandmother could tell of the strangest things; things that happened in Ireland a long, long time ago. She could tell of goblins and dwarfs that lived in the mountains in back of their farm, and of dreadful dragons that roared with tongues of fire. "One must remember that when one talks of such horrible things they are never very far away," Grandmother said. Then the children sighed in delighted horror, and felt goose bumps creep, cold and chilling, down their backs.

"Tell more about the vikings, Grandmother."

Grandmother shook her head. "I don't know any more about the vikings than what the people here in the country village have to tell. And no one can know for sure how much of that is truth or exaggeration. Wives cackle like scared hens, and men bellow like dumb oxen when they talk about the vikings. Not a sensible word to get out of anyone!"

"Brother Cormac has told about the vikings," Patric enthusiastically broke in. "They are some awful northern warriors. Their ships sail faster than the wind and look like huge, monstrous dragons. They attack like lightning from a clear heaven and steal and plunder everything they can carry with them. And then suddenly, they are gone again."

"That is pure witchcraft!" Sunniva said excitedly.

"The vikings have a sword that can cut stone, and arrows that fly faster than lightning," said Moira. "That is what the miller's wife says."

"They have the teeth of beasts of prey and horns on their foreheads," whispered Cara. "And they eat children alive...or at least they take them as prisoners."

"And they swear all the time," Roderic stuttered through the opening where he had lost two baby teeth. That was the worst thing that he could think of to say, on the spur of the moment like this. Grandmother Gaelion whinnied softly. "I can tell that you are all good listeners, at least when you're in town."

"Now, you tell us of the vikings, Grandmother," Sunniva begged.

"We will have to wait until the morning. I hear someone coming that doesn't like me to ruin your night's sleep." She tousled Roderic's hair. "Tomorrow we will trick the rooster and get up before he has time to even shake his wings. In bed with you all now!"

They scampered across the earthen floor and were already tucked under their skin rugs before mother set the buckets down outside of the door. She quickly peeked into the room. "Are they all asleep?"

"Yes, they are," whispered Grandmother Gaelion back to her. "Sleeping as soundly as rocks. Such good children...."

And that was nearly the truth, for only Patric lay awake. He heard his father come, tramping into the house, settling his wooden axe down in the corner and pulling the heavy wooden bar across the door. Grandmother Gaelion snored soundly in her bench bed. Through the smoke hole in the ceiling, he could see the evening turning into black night. Patric lay listening to the sound of the waves hitting the rocks on the shore, until he also fell sound asleep.

In the country village, the stories of the vikings grew more savage and cruel with each passing day. The feared warriors from the north had swarmed over most of the world, they were told, plundering, ravaging and murdering. They stole the holy relics from the monasteries and churches.

The vikings began their raids many years before. They started attacking monasteries in Lindisfarne in England and Iona on the east coast of Scotland. Rumours of the many riches to be found there spread north. Every year new ships sailed out. Some of the vikings had settled on the Orkney Islands and the Shetland Islands and built their empires there. From those areas ships sailed into the Irish sea to plunder and ravage.

That summer, neighbours came often for visits during the evening. As the sun slowly sank in back of the hills, they gathered around the long table and talked with quick, whispering voices.

In the wide bed in the corner of the room, the children lay quietly, pretending to be asleep. No one noticed the five pairs of wide eyes peeking through a little split in the skin rug. It was terribly exciting to hear the tales the grown-ups had to tell. But such things only happened to others, of course, and far, far away from this peaceful little corner of Ireland.

Then, one day, the tales turned into reality.

"The monastery is burning!" their father shouted.

Everyone in the room jumped up from their places. Cups of soup bounced on the floor.

Father was pale. He pointed towards the west. Tongues of fire licked up towards the sky over the tall church tower. The huge oak trees in the monastery garden were surrounded by crackling bronze flames. The sky suddenly darkened with birds fleeing from their nests.

"What's happening?" Mother shrieked. She covered her face with her hands. The smallest children pressed themselves, like frightened animals, against her frock.

It was then that Patric discovered the black ships down on the shore. They resembled dragons in an evil and horrifying fable. The prows stretched tall with huge, gaping mouths.

The vikings!

Father fetched the sharp farmer's axe he always had in back of the door. "So, that pack of robbers have reached our shores. I'll show them!"

But his arms dropped. Vikings swarmed out of the ships like ants. The shores were soon covered by these warring robbers, armed with spears, axes and gleaming swords. It would be useless to fight. He threw the axe down.

"In the name of God and all the saints of Ireland!" Mother called. "They are carrying away all of the treasures in the monastery, the holy books and boxes."

At that moment, Grandmother Gaelion came across the yard with an armful of hay. When she saw the warriors on the shore, she dropped the hay and shouted. "And I have bread in the oven! I'll be damned if this mob of thieves is going to get a taste of my good bread!" She turned and ran towards the baking house, but Father caught her by the arm. "We have to get out of here. We haven't a moment to spare. They will be here soon!"

And so they ran. Grandmother Gaelion limped beside them with her cane. Father carried Moira on his shoulders. Mother dragged and pulled Cara with her. Patric and Sunniva took little Roderic between them. They ran as fast as their legs could carry them, stumbling on rocks and tree stalks, getting up again. Branches slashed their faces and their hands and nails were bloody from scratching and clutching their way up the rocky slopes. The whole time, the sounds of weapons resounded in their ears. The air was filled with the pungent smell of smoke from the burning monastery. They raced towards a hill top in the forest, where there was a secret cave, a cave in which the children used to hide when playing robbers. The opening was camouflaged with branches and ferns, and no one would find them there if they just sat perfectly still.... But then Sunniva suddenly shouted, "Stella! Stella is tied in the barn!"

Patric stopped abruptly. Her shout punctured his brain. All of the air went out of his lungs. Stella had to be saved. She must not burn to death in the barn.

"Run after Mother and Father. Hurry!" he said as he pushed little Roderic forward. Patric turned and ran after Sunniva. Her red hair flew like a fan around her head as she raced down the hill. Was their father calling their names? They were not conscious of anything other than the blood pumping hard and hurting in their chests, and the fact that they had to continue.

They stopped to catch their breath when they reached the stone fence. Blood froze to ice when they discovered the warriors were closing in on their farm. But they could not turn back. They stooped down and crept into the low-raftered barn. Their little colt stood bowed over a pile of sweet clover. Good little horse! They pulled and drew on the ropes. Finally the knot loosened.

Sunniva spied out of the window in the barn door. "I'm so scared," she whispered. The vikings had come right into the farmyard. And they did not have horns nor did they have the sharp teeth of predatory animals like Miriam had said, but they still looked fearsome in their heavy warrior gear. Their weapons, steel helmets and shields gleamed in the sun. One of them bellowed nastily when he could not find anything of worth in their little hut.

He emptied Mother's jewellery chest and her one brooch rolled out onto the ground. The whole farm yard smelled of burnt bread. One of the warriors roared, "We'll burn more than just bread!" And he lifted his torch under the edge of the roof. The dry thatched roof burned readily.

At that same moment, Patric and Sunniva pushed the little colt through the back door and out of the barn. They raced across the field. This was a matter of life and death! Run, Stella, run! Oh, if only Stella had been a grown horse, so she could have carried them both to safety!

Then it happened. They were just a few paces from the stone fence when Sunniva stumbled on a branch. A short cry escaped her lips as she hit the ground, and the man with the torch saw them. He shouted a sharp command. Everything went so fast that afterwards Patric could only remember short pictures: the horse that pulled itself free of them, whinnying and then disappearing into the brush; men with their threatening axes who tied their hands and arms so tightly that the ropes cut into their skin.

They were dragged towards the ship on the shore. They stumbled beside the monastery walls where the vikings were carrying the last of the heavy chests out from the church. Brown figures in monk's robes lay just outside of the stone walls, completely still, with strangely distorted faces and pools of red blood beneath their necks.

The men sat at their oars, ready. As soon as the command was shouted, the men rowed so vigorously, water foamed against the bow. Once out in the open sea, they hoisted the huge square sail. It cracked and flapped in the breeze. Wild, jubilant shouts rang over the sea. Their plundering expedition had been successful.

Patric and Sunniva were stiff with shock. They stared back at the bay that their mother had called God's forgotten corner of St. Patric's green island. Many of the farms were in flames and directly over the monastery hung clouds of rolling, threatening smoke.

"Do you see anything up there?" whispered Sunniva.

Patric looked towards the place where the secret cave was. For a moment he thought he caught sight of his mother's white scarf. But no. Everything was quiet.

And then they were pushed into the innermost part of the ship's tent. The wind blew towards the northeast.

Night and day melted into one. They slept on deck scaffolds, cramped into the space between barrels that smelled sourly of rotten fish and sea water. There were many prisoners. An English girl cried out to her mother in the dark, and men wailed in foreign languages. From a dark corner came the voice of a monk reciting long prayers in Latin: *In nomine Patris et Filii et Spiritus Sancti....*

Patric snuggled closely into his sister. Thus far, Sunniva had just been a bothersome little girl, hanging at his heels wherever he went and stood. Now he discovered how very glad he was to have his sister. Her small hand was comforting to hold, and it seemed reassuring and safe to hear her breathe so near his own face. It was just the two of them against the whole great and foreign world. Neither of them knew what was going to happen. It was as if their whole future also floated away on this great and open sea.

The viking ship rose and sank on the mighty waves. Somewhere in the middle of the sea, the wind blew up. It wailed and the sea growled and boomed against the sides of the ship. The huge square sail suddenly pounded against the mast as if it would tear loose any minute. The monk stopped praying and grumbled, "Good thing that the vikings have tied us up like this or we would surely be washed overboard. May God reward them for their thoughtfulness!"

The prisoners struggled, holding themselves in place as the ship tilted from side to side. Patric bruised himself against the edge of one of the barrels, and his head felt feverish and heavy. Several times he had to turn aside and throw up. Good thing I am not hungry, he thought ironically. No one gets any food here anyway.

How long he lay there, he did not know. Every time he closed his eyes the same nightmare lurked. He was in a bitterly cold land, way up in the north, where predatory animals prowled in the dark forests. It was not until the ship came into smooth waters that he fell into a long, peaceful sleep. In this dream, he thought someone was cutting loose the ropes that tied his hands. When he finally opened his eyes, he discovered that his hands were indeed free, and that daylight filtered across the deck.

Such a strange land, thought Patric, as he stood on the ship's deck. Mountains rose sharply into the heavens, grey-blue and mighty. Here and there, a waterfall spilled out from a mountainside into the bay, which lay at the base of the mountain, green and smooth like a dragon's eye. Clusters of summer-brown log houses were tucked into the furthest corner of the inlet, sunning themselves in the clear water.

Sunniva drew in the fresh air, feeling that she would never get enough. "Where are we?" she whispered to the English monk.

"In Norway," he answered. "The home of the Norwegians and the vikings." His words hit her like a cold gust of air. "May the angels and all of the saints protect us. From here it is impossible to get home alive."

As the ship neared land, they saw that the shores were swarming with people, shouting and hollering in a strange language, waving their arms. As soon as the plank was lowered, women rushed onto the ship. They threw themselves around the necks of their men and laughed and cried. They acted like a flock of cows just let out of the barn in the spring. Blond children clung to the legs of the men. They begged for a look into the chests.

The men were in good humour. One of them opened the largest, iron-bound chest. Oh, oooooooooh, such a glitter of gold and treasure! The children were each given a piece of silver, and then the man threw down the lid again. "Out of my way, children!"

The warriors ploughed their way through the crowds of people and lifted the chests up on the backs of some small, ragged horses that were waiting. Then this strange gathering trailed up between the log houses. The prisoners walked after them, only two dark-skinned men were back on the boat. No one ever saw them again.

The path wound through a forest. Wind whistled through the tall fir trees. It had just rained, so the ground was saturated with puddles of water. The little English girl tripped several times, but a warrior picked her up again with an angry grunt. Patric dragged his feet in the mud and thought of golden brown bread, newly churned butter, and crisp mutton.

When they came out of the forest, they saw a whole little town spread out before them, with farm houses and green and gold-coloured fields surrounding them almost like a chess board. Patric was astonished, because for one or another reason he had imagined that these viking warriors lived in stone castles upon mountain tops. But the place they were headed towards did resemble a castle in some ways. It was an immense farm situated at the top of the valley, so that it seemed to look down upon the village with arrogance. There were so many houses in the large farmyard that one could barely count them all, and there were guards and warriors everywhere. One of the guards grabbed a torch that lit the walls of the houses in the twilight. He led the prisoners to a low stone hut, situated on the furthest edge of the farm yard, right next to a marsh. He drew the bar from the door and signalled for them to go in and find a place to sleep inside.

Patric and Sunniva stood, staring into the dark room. People were sleeping all over the floor, breathing heavily and turning in their sleep. They fumbled to an empty place in the corner and, exhausted, sank down on the earthen floor. But it was impossible to sleep. Hunger writhed and tore at their insides. They sniffed and cried, both of them.

Then Patric felt a hand on his shoulder. "My name is Una," someone whispered. "I hear that you have come from the west some place. I do not know your language well, but I have picked up a few words from all of the others that have come and gone here in this house." Her voice was soft and confiding. "I will find some bread for you both."

She picked up a coal from the fire and lit a stone lamp that was filled with fish oil. The light flickered across her high cheek bones and thick, flaxen hair, and as she got up they could see by her round stomach that she was pregnant. She rummaged in a little hole in the wall and found some dry bread crusts.

"I am tired and have to get some sleep," she whispered. "But eat now. I do not have much else to offer you." She blew out the flame. Never had food tasted better. It nearly tasted better than the fine, white cakes that Grandmother Gaelion baked for the holidays at home in Ireland.

The next day, they were taken to the great hall. "This is nearly as nice as the monastery church at home," Sunniva whispered as she clutched her brother's arm. "But I can't say that I like it here at all."

The hall was at least forty paces long. The room was lit by four long pits of fire. At the furthest end, several girls were busy grilling a whole animal over the open flames. The tantalizing smell of roasted meat swirled up between the rafters and out through the smoke hole in the ceiling. The log walls were covered with colourful hangings woven in strange patterns. And between the hangings and over the iron-studded oak door hung weapons, more weapons than they had ever seen before. Patric shuddered in fright. Under the rows of sharp-edged axes and swords, he saw a group of men playing a board game. They reminded him, in a very ominous way, of a flock of helpless, mindless crows that had their wings clipped. None of these men could any longer go out on viking raids. Some of them just had stumps instead of legs, and others had no arms.

"Closer!" a sharp voice commanded. Right in the middle of the long wall sat a man on an ornately carved, high-backed chair. His face was frightening. A wide, blue-white scar curved across his face from his forehead to the root of his nose, and then down into his black beard. The mark of a fierce sword stroke.

Beside this man sat a woman in a blue silk smock. Patric could not take his eyes from her. Her face was as white as the scarf she had around her head. On her waist she had a silver belt, and it was not difficult to see that she was as round and bulky as Una. On her belt hung a heavy ring of keys. But what caught Patric's attention was a little gilt Irish brooch fastened at her neckline.

The man rose from his high seat, his eyes gleaming like cold steel. He pointed to the silver rings and coins piled before him on the table. "Is this all you bring back with you after a whole summer of viking raids?" he railed at the warriors. "Do you think that I give you ships, weapons and equipment so that you can amuse yourselves with Frankish women and bathe in the sea!"

It was so quiet in the great hall that Patric could hear his own breathing. The man grasped a handwritten book that was laying on the table before him. He quickly turned the pages. There were many wonderful drawings, but he could not understand anything of the writing. He threw the book into the fire. The flames consumed the book as quickly as the mouth of a furious dragon. Patric barely managed to stop himself from shouting. In the red firelight he could see, as in a dream, Brother Cormac as he sat bowed over a calfskin, painting and drawing with minute precision, in all the colours of the rainbow.

The man raised his eyes slowly and reviewed the prisoners. The English monk and a couple of the other men seemed to be stout and strong. He did not pay much attention to the little English girl, clinging to her mother in fright.

And then he caught sight of Patric and Sunniva. He laughed and tousled their hair. Never had he seen anything to compare with the colour of their hair in this part of the world.

"Are you Irish?" he asked them, in their own language.

"Yes, sir."

"Ireland is a fine little island. The whole land is like one huge chest of treasure that never seems to empty."

He scrutinized Patric from head to foot. "How old are you?"

"Eleven winters, sire."

"And you?"

"Ten summers."

Sunniva had always been an exceptionally brave little girl. She had been the one to help her mother with calving, and she was not afraid to go out, even if it was pitch dark in the yard. But Patric was both astounded and horrified when he saw her straighten up and say, "Our names are Patric and Sunniva, and we are the oldest children on the Neal farm. Our father is a free Irish farmer."

Her voice shook as she raised her arm and pointed at his lady's enormous bust line. "That brooch is my mother's. I am absolutely sure of that, because it has been in our family for a long time. I saw your warriors empty her jewellery chest. St. Patric will punish you all for such thievery!"

Silence filled the hall. The man in the high seat lifted his eyebrows in amazement. And then he threw his head back and laughed. His laughter reminded them of the howl of a sick dog. "Your mother will get her brooch back. But not until next summer. Then I will go to Ireland myself!"

This answer seemed to amuse the warriors, as laughter rang through the hall. Even the man's wife laughed heartily as she held her round stomach. "I am sure I will have use for this lively girl. I will remember her when the time comes."

"What do you think she meant by that?" Sunniva whispered.

Patric shook his head. He was scared to death that Sunniva would say something more and make the vikings roar at her.

The man stood up and took two long strides out to the middle of the floor. He positioned himself directly in front of the children, legs wide apart and arms crossed before his chest. They could see amusement in his sharp eyes. But he said, "You can forget your fine Irish names now that you are here in this land. From now on your names are Reim and Tir. They are names that are more suited to slaves."

And so they were called Reim and Tir, and they were slaves. They repeated their names over and over as they trudged across the yard to the grey stone hut where the slaves lived. Reim and Tir. Slave names. It was as if they could not get this vicious truth into their heads. But the slave guard that hurried them across the yard and into the little room was real enough: a broad, tall viking with a stiff goat's beard.

The fire crackled on the hearth. Una stirred around and around in a huge pot with hearty strokes. She stood over the fire, her face as red and gleaming as a full moon. Lifting one hand, she stroked a few wet hairs back from her forehead.

"Isn't that porridge ready yet?" came a hearty cry. "My stomach is howling like a hungry wolf. If you take any longer, you will fall asleep and drop into the pot, girl!"

Laughter and chuckling came from the dark corners. Some of the slaves sat on a bench and leaned towards the warmth of the hearth. Others sat on the hard, trampled clay floor with wooden bowls balancing between their knees. An old man, who had given up waiting, lay sleeping in some hay. He snored loudly and talked quietly to himself in his sleep.

The slave children stood hidden behind of the poles that held the roof up. They moved around uneasily when they saw Una's eyes darken to look like bits of coal under her kerchief. She was not above sending her wooden spoon right across the room if she was irritated. But this time she answered, "Don't get cheeky with me, or you just might get the answer you deserve! Come here with your bowl, Digralde!"

The giant got up from his bench, nearly hitting his head on the rafters. In the glow of the firelight he looked unreal. His woolly neck and stooping body reminded the children of a burly bear. He thrust his wooden bowl towards her. "Fill it to the top. You can't fill up Digralde with just a couple of small spoonfuls. And you wouldn't give me burnt porridge, would you, Una?"

"Pigs aren't usually fussy, if they are really hungry," Una grinned. She ladled a worthy portion into his bowl, as the other men stood waiting restlessly. Then the women and the old people came in turn. The tantalizing aroma from the pot was unbearable. Finally, the children also came forth. As soon as their bowls were filled, they darted back to their places like small rats.

Suddenly a roar filled the room. The huge bear of a man jumped up from his bench, hopping around and around on one foot. He threatened Una with his fists, "Ow, ow, you burned me, you darned witch of a woman!" He held his throat with both hands, his tongue wiggling at them like some kind of a farm dog. His bowl fell to the floor with a thud.

"I told you that the porridge was hot," Una laughed. The children crept up against the walls, trying to make themselves invisible. Digralde must be like the god that they believed in here; the one named Thor, who could get so mad that he made sparks fly in the air with his hammer.

The giant sat on his knees, sweeping the spilled porridge back into his bowl with his hands. Then he sat down on the bench again and carefully laid his enormous arms around his bowl of porridge as if guarding a great treasure, his eyes just barely visible over the edge of the bowl, greedy and bloodshot. The other slaves slurped and smacked, so the room was filled with sounds. Some of the men sat on their knees right in front of their bowls, their noses buried in the wonderful porridge. Their beards looked as if they were frosted. There was no great difference between this group of people and a litter of pigs. If they had not been so hungry, they probably would have laughed at the sight of themselves.

Some of the young boys tried to steal an extra spoonful of porridge. But Una quickly hit them on the fingers with her wooden spoon. She had to save a bit of porridge for old Klegge, too.

She walked across the room and shook the pile of rags on the floor. Klegge had hay in his hair and beard. His eyes squinted as he peered into the room, struggling to pull himself up on his elbow.

"It must be evening, for I smell porridge. I thank the goddesses of fortune for that. And then I think I will lay down for a little nap again afterwards, ha, ha.

It is better to sleep without pay than it is to slave without pay."

Una held his spoon for him and pushed the porridge between his toothless gums. "Use your mouth to eat with now, dear old man."

Klegge kept still for a while. He slurped and ate. And then he patted his stomach and sighed heavily. "Porridge doesn't keep you full very long. But still, porridge is the only food slaves and small farmers have every single day. But up there," he said, nodding his head towards the great hall, "up there, the earl and his wife sit, fattening themselves upon meat and fowl and bread made of the finest grain. And what they do not manage to eat up, they give to their dogs!"

"I would not mind drinking wine out of their golden horns and dancing my feet off in the earl's great hall," said one of the young men. His name was Vidur and he was Una's brother. He tried to pull one of the young slave girls out onto the floor. She stuck her tongue out at him and laughed, "Ya, that would be quite a sight!"

Digralde gasped in a great yawn. "It is a good thing we don't have far to go to find a place to sleep after a meal of porridge." He sank back onto the bench and fell asleep momentarily. The others moved away from him. Klegge's snoring was a mere cradle song compared to Digralde's thundering snore. The slaves packed hay into their ears to deafen the noise and rolled over towards the wall. Before a shimmering light spread across the eastern sky, a new day would begin.

Part II

*R*eim felt uneasy. Tonight it has to happen, he thought, otherwise there will be no other chances to get away. In the dark room, he caught sight of Digralde's heavy form. He sat leaning against the rock wall, and Reim knew that he was sharply alert. He listened for every movement in the leaves, every branch that cracked, every noise that might differ from the familiar noises of the air and forest.

He had been a slave a whole year now, Reim thought. And he might just end his life as a slave, too. Tir lay beside him in the hay, fast asleep, her face bright in the pale moonlight. Once her name had been Sunniva; once she had been the daughter of an Irish farmer. She was a lively, freckled girl, this sister whom he had fought with and had so much fun with at home in Ireland. She did not resemble that girl now. She had become thin and bony, her cheeks were sunken and her hair hung in red tufts around her face.

Reim curled tightly into his sister. Through the smoke hole he could see a piece of the sky. There were heavy, dark clouds. Every now and then, the clouds parted, and the cold face of the moon stared down at him. Is the moon filled with good or bad omens tonight, Reim wondered. Kumba would have known, but Kumba was asleep. "Just let me stay here," she had said. "My destiny is with this farm, where I have lived my whole life."

Reim closed his eyes, and his thoughts drifted away like heavy clouds in the dark heaven.

His first period in this new land had been a nightmare. "Try and be brave," a voice deep inside him said. "Show them that you are a proud Irish farmer's son."

But that helped so little. All that he had been through had solidified into one big clump of ice in his chest. He was afraid. He was afraid of the warriors that kept watch everywhere, afraid of the rough men slaves, afraid of everything foreign and unknown.

But worst of all, he was lonely and he longed to go home. He bore this homesickness with him day and night. Deep inside he carried an image of their dear little farm home in Ireland. Often, he smelled freshly baked bread, and saw his stooped Grandmother Gaelion. If he heard laughter, he immediately thought of his brothers and sisters at home. Tears sprang from his eyes, and if he quickly glanced at Tir, he could see that she felt just the same.

One evening, she came over to him and whispered, "Come, I have something to show you." They sneaked past the watch posts and ran down the path to the shore. Suddenly, Tir was gone, having disappeared into the thin air.

"Look! Here I am," she whispered secretively. "Way up here in a tree!"

Reim took hold of a branch in the huge fir tree and climbed up to the top where Tir sat. He held fast and slid over until he could hold onto the tree trunk. "If this branch breaks...."

"It won't break," Tir answered, laughing. Her hair blew freely in the wind. Beneath them, the cliff walls dropped right into the green-black water. The sight of the immense, open sea was breathtaking. It was as if they could see the whole world. They saw thousands of islands and rock reefs, and the light blue strip where the ocean meets the heavens. A long way out in the ocean they could see a large island that was greener that any of the other islands. Tir waved her arms and shouted, "And there you see Ireland!" Reim quickly grabbed her with both hands so she would not fall.

"Silly," Una said when they came back to the farm and told of what they had seen. "You will have to travel much further than the islands in the bay to get to your homeland. The ocean is not just some puddle, you know." She laughed. "But you probably won't understand that until you have sailed between all the islands and rock reefs out there. Wise old folk say that the ocean is enormous. And some tell of a sea monster that is out there, that twines itself around all of the islands, biting itself in the tail. I would like to know if that is true or not, but none of us slaves have ever been outside of the bay area."

"Do you believe what Una said?" Tir whispered as they lay on their straw beds that evening.

"What, about the sea monster?"

"No, about Ireland."

"Not a bit," Reim whispered back.

But after this, it became an unwritten law between them to hide their precious memories deep inside, and talk as little as possible to others about their homeland.

The earl, Håkon, was mighty. He owned many farms. He owned ships, animals and slaves. When he travelled from farm to farm on inspection, he had a whole flock of warriors with him—several hundred men.

The earl had more power than any other man in the area. Yes, more powerful than anyone in the whole district. After him ranked the yeomen that had sat on their own ancestral farms for many generations. Then came the farmers on the smaller farms. Many farmers swore an oath of loyalty to the earl. They provided an overflow of food and drink for the earl and his warriors as they travelled through their villages. In return, they hoped that the earl would protect and defend them if their villages were attacked by enemies or thieves.

The slaves were absolutely the lowest on this ladder of rank. They had no rights. On a middle-sized farm, there were usually only one or two slaves, and the farmer worked just as hard as the slaves. But there was no doubt as to who was free and who was not free. Earl Håkon had more than thirty slaves and servants. He had appointed one of his warriors as slave guard. That guard was Orm Viking, a tall man with a goat's beard and a very little head planted on a very thick neck. Orm had been on many viking raids during his youth, and as most of the men who had gone through many raids, his mind had turned evil. The slaves thought that he owned up to his name, Orm, which in the language of the viking land meant snake. He lay in wait, watching, like a snake with his cunning tongue and sly, black, beady eyes.

"The pig pen is the right place for a slave boy like you," Orm sneered, twitching Reim's ear. "Get going now. Off with you. And do a good job of it!"

Reim wrinkled his nose the first few days. The pig pen was muddy and filthy, and smelled atrocious. He forced himself to think of what his Grandmother Gaelion had said to him, home in Ireland, when he had to weed the thistles out of the garden patch: "One can get used to anything, both sour and salt."

At least it was warm in the pig pen, and he did not mind the smell after he had been there a while. It wasn't long before he felt that he knew each pig and rather liked having them around. The largest sow had just given birth to eight pink piglets. The last piglet to come into the world was so thin and sickly that Reim carried it inside his coat to keep it warm. He could watch it grow, day by day. Soon the little piglet grunted and snorted with its strange snout and rolled around in the mud. When Reim was depressed and sat sulking in the innermost corner of the pig pen, the little piglet would waddle over to him and gaze at him with its bright, black eyes as if to say, "We lead one filthy life, don't we?" And then Reim had to laugh and scratch the pig's neck.

On a stool beside him, Reim had a pile of walrus hides that had arrived with a merchant ship from the north. He cut the hides into strips with a sharp knife, and then braided them into ropes. Old Klegge had shown him how to do this. His fingers were too stiff now for that kind of work.

"In the spring, the earl will venture out on new viking raids westward," Orm Viking said. "And we have to have the ships readied by then."

That meant that Reim had to braid ropes for the ships, day after day, for weeks and months on end.

Tir worked with the other slave women.

During her first days in this new land, she had wondered about the strange songs she heard. She could not distinguish where they were coming from. The tones rose and fell, rose and fell, until far into the evening hours.

Now she knew. The song came from the mill. The women had their own song down there. Every day they did the same heavy, monotonous work. And every day they sang the same monotone song. And now Tir was one of them.

In the morning, she would glance quickly at the pale daylight sifting through the smoke hole in the roof of the slaves' quarters. She would pull on her smock and eat a few pieces of bread before fetching some water from the barrel in the corner of the room. She would throw a few drops of cold water on her face and then hurry, shivering, after the other women, down the well-worn patch to the house by the waterfalls. She always ran the last part of the way. It was good to come in under a roof. Even though it was never warm in the mill, there was always a glow from the hearth to keep the grain from freezing.

Inside the mill, a great grey rock dominated the floor space. It resembled the enormous gape of a troll.

The rocks worked like two great chewing jaws, grinding and crushing the grain to flour. It was impossible to budge the rocks if all of the women did not push at exactly the same time.

So every morning, Tir took her place, and they all pushed with all of their might. Ooooooooooooooo ohhhhh! Then the mill started moving. It grated and scraped like the broken voice of an old man, grinding and grinding. Clouds of fine flour filled the air.

The women sang. Old, grey-haired Kumba led the singing. She had spent her whole life treading around and around in this same circle. Una sang with a high voice, just a bit-off key. Beside her, walked two dark-skinned girls. They sang in a language that Tir did not understand. The little English girl clung closely to her mother's skirts, but she moved her lips to the song also. The only one that did not sing was a slave women from Frankland, Yrsa. She walked in the outermost ring in order to keep an eye on her little child, a wild, light-haired boy of two years. The mother had trouble keeping him away from the flour bins. Every chance he got, he filled his mouth with flour. He giggled and laughed and smeared the flour over his whole face all the way up to his fair hair.

At times, Una could not resist laughing at this precious, wild child. But Yrsa quickly retorted, "Just wait until it is your turn!"

Una fell into thought for a moment as she stroked her own round stomach. But then she resolutely pushed on.

Digralde was the father of the child that Una carried. Everyone was quite certain of that, because when he thought that no one was looking, he would sneak over to Una and pat her stomach. Then they both laughed and fooled around a bit as Una rubbed her nose against his bearded chin. "Oh, to be free," Digralde would say, as he stared into the glowing ashes in the evening. "If I only had been free and had a little farm on the side of a sun-filled slope. Not a big farm, just a piece of land, a cow, a couple of goats and most of all, I would like a horse. And then a worthy wife, ha, ha, ha...."

Klegge stirred the ashes with a branch. "Don't waste your time on dreams," he said acidly. "I am old enough to know the meaning of the laws. And it is written that no slave may own anything more than a sharp knife!"

Digralde's face darkened. He drew his knife and held it threateningly out in front of him. "I have carried more than my share of work on another man's farm for more than fifteen years. I have slaved and toiled without ever receiving more for my work than the straw sack that I sleep on and a meal of porridge when my stomach was howling for solid food. And whose fault is that? My own father's, I tell you. If I ever get a hold of him, this little slave's knife is going to be put to good use!"

Una ran to his side and quieted him. "Calm down now, Digralde. Don't you see that you are frightening the children?"

Digralde stuck his knife back in his belt again, standing boldly in the middle of the room. "I am not a weak child any longer," he shouted. "I know how to get my freedom!"

There was an astounded silence in the slave quarters. Everyone stared at Digralde. They could not have been more surprised if Digralde had said that he was to be the next king.

One day, a girl stood on the other side of the rock fence near the slave quarters. She was clothed in rags. Her feet were bound in rags and she had a fringed shawl thrown over her brown braids. She pulled and tugged at a stubborn cow that refused to follow her.

"Dumb cow," she scolded, thrashing the cow with a branch. "Please move just a bit, you monstrous ogre of an animal!"

But the cow played dumb. She planted all four of her feet firmly on the ground and sent her tail up in the air. And there she stood. Immovable.

"We can help you!"

Tir jumped over the rock fence, with Reim following close behind. The girl in the rag smock pulled and tugged with all of her might and the other two pushed from behind.

"If you spit into your hands and say tvi, maybe she will move," Tir suggested.

"Mooooooooooooo," the cow bellowed in answer, and slapped them in the face with her tail. The little girl gave up, placed her hands on her hips and laughed.

"Where are you a slave?" Reim asked. He struggled a bit with the Norse language.

"I am certainly not a slave!" she exclaimed. The girl pointed to a spot on the rock strewn slope. "I live there, together with my mother and my brothers. Three bandits let out our cow, so I had to chase her over the whole countryside. I did not get a hold of her tail until I had run all the way up this rocky slope."

Reim looked through the trees to see if he could find the farm the girl was talking about. A thin, grey strip of smoke rose through the fir trees down in the valley. There could not be a real house down there. It was as if the smoke rose directly out of the earth.

The girl told them that her name was Tora. And then she asked where they came from, since they spoke with such a strange dialect. Tir and Reim both talked at once; about their farm in Ireland and the burning of the monastery, about the monks that were killed, and about the vikings that had forced them aboard their viking ship and made them their slaves.

Tora kicked loose a rock, sending it rolling and bouncing down the steep hill. "The chieftains and great landowners are all alike. They do not care about anything other than their warring and fighting. And if things do not turn out right for them, they take it out on us poor folk!"

Then she told them her story. Two summers ago, the district had been attacked by the Illuges. The earl's family and the Illuge family had been in opposition since the creation of the world. They sneered and growled at the sight of each other. As soon as one was killed, the others pledged revenge. And their revenge always called for bloodshed.

She was out in the pasture with her mother and smaller brothers the day the warriors attacked their village. They saw flames licking over the tops of the fir trees and managed to keep hidden until evening. When they returned, their little farm had been reduced to ashes. And their father lay dead in the yard. He had been cut down by the warriors.

Afterwards, they had managed day by day. But they had had to build their sod hut on the north slope and their fields were just a jumble of rock and stone. And they only had this cow and one skinny, old goat. Tora shrugged, "Maybe one day, we will just walk away from it all."

"Leave? But where would you go?"

"To Iceland! A land that lies just a few days travel by ship across the great sea. Folk say that there is enough land for everyone there, with green fields as far as the eye can see. But I have heard that there are terrible trolls and spirits there," Tora said, as she shivered. "They say that the water boils right out of the earth, and that there are bubbling and boiling troll pots everywhere. But I don't know if I can believe everything that people say."

They heard a voice call out from the area where they saw the blue smoke rising.

"That is mother calling *Redlin*," Tora said. "I had better hold on tightly now!" She grabbed the cow's tail, and together they ran down the stony hill, sending rocks flying in all directions after them.

Tir was usually so exhausted after a day's work that she crumbled like a rag doll on her bedding of straw. But one evening, she leaned over to Reim and said, "Something strange happened to me today. I met the son of the earl."

It happened as she started home from the mill. Suddenly she heard the stamping of a horse on the path behind her, so she stepped aside. She was relieved to see that it was just one of the small, heather-coloured horses that were so common in this land. Upon the horse's back sat a light-haired boy dressed in blue.

"Oh, what a lovely horse," she exclaimed as she patted it. The horse was stout and strong and had a coarse mane and wise, shining eyes. Tir was filled with such a longing for her own dear colt that she had played with back home in Ireland.

Then she looked up at the fair-haired boy on the horse's back. He had a little upturned nose and so many freckles that they looked as though someone had sprayed his face with tar. His eyes were the same colour as his well-made blue cloak, which was held together by a belt with a silver buckle. On his chest shone a brooch with the pattern of a snake. His dress was certainly different in comparison to the plain russet smocks the slaves wore every day.

"Who are you?" Tir asked in amazement.

The boy straightened up tall on the back of his horse.

"I am the son of the earl, Håkon, who was the son of Sigtrygg Silkeskjegg who fought at Serkland, son of Hallvard Herse who conquered two armies in one battle, son of Lodve Lovspake who was a law man at the courts, son of Inge Istermage who fought against the Illuge family and who is buried in that huge grave mound in the yard, son of Bjørn Berserk who came over the mountains from the east and settled here with his people. His decedents have always been among the most powerful in this land."

Tir was speechless. The boy had named all of his ancestors without as much as blinking his eyes. It sounded like a shepherd just naming his sheep, or possibly more like one of the monks at home when they recited their whole mass in Latin.

She wiped her nose with the back of her hand. "I can only remember one name in my whole ancestry, my grandmother, Gaelion. She can really bake bread and churn butter. And she knows hundreds of tales and legends," Tir said.

"You can't remember more names because you are just a slave. Slaves don't have ancestors that are rich or powerful."

That made her so angry that she stamped her foot on the ground. "Rich, we have never been! But you can mind my words, we are not of slave descent! My ancestors have always been free farmers. My brother and I were stolen from our farm in Ireland by your father's skinflint warriors. Thieves and murderers, you are, all of you!"

The boy laughed. "And next year it will be my turn."

"What do you mean?"

"Next year I will be twelve winters old. Then I have to go out on viking raids for the first time to plunder gold and silver and treasure."

"And slaves, like me?"

The boy shrugged his shoulders. "What else can the son of an earl do?" He kicked his horse in the shins and pulled up on the reins.

"Take me with you on your ship," Tir pleaded. "Take me with you back to Ireland!"

But both the horse and the blue cloak had already disappeared into the thick forest.

Besides Reim and Tir, there were six other slave children at the farm. The youngest was Yrsa's quick young son. His mother had her hands full just keeping track of him. Given a chance, he would climb upon the bench and jump right into the flour bin. Then he threw flour by the handfuls up into the air, so it would sprinkle down on him again like soft, light snow.

His mother shook him soundly. "You little rascal! What do you think the earl's wife will say if she sees you do that?"

But in the end, she could not help but laugh. He looked so comical, his little beady eyes blinking mischievously through a blanket of white flour.

The three bigger boys in the slave quarters were not counted as slave children any longer. They were between the ages of twelve and fifteen winters old—no one knew exactly. Their names were Lut, Leggjalde and Hosve and they had been born slaves. They were sluggish and lazy, as people usually become when they live their whole lives in bondage. The youngest, Hosve, had been whipped and badgered until he would jump in fright at the sound of Orm Viking's voice, as a beaten dog under his master.

And then there were the two dark-skinned girls with glittering eyes and teeth as white as the glacier mountains. Their names were Muna and Ofarim and they came all the way from Arabia. They had been captured by the vikings that came to their land to plunder silk and spices. Earl Håkon had bought the girls at a slave market in Denmark. He often asked them to come to the great hall to tell him stories of the strange, foreign land they came from. He was greatly amused by their tales of strange horses that had humps on their backs and hardly ever drank water.

The light-haired English girl had been captured with her mother near a town called York. No one had ever heard her story, as she was very quiet and refused to talk. She walked with her head bowed constantly. No one could understand what she had to sulk about, because she at least had her own mother with her. But they soon knew. The girl was sick. She grew paler and weaker each day, and one day she cried when she had to go to the mill. She fell back onto the straw on the floor as she tried to get up in the morning. Her mother prayed for her, and Kumba fetched her magical herbs and cooked a warm broth for her. But neither sorcery nor Christian prayers helped. The little girl died one bitterly cold night as the first snow started to drift over the land. Digralde bowed his head and went out to dig in the frozen earth. A few days later, he had to go out again to dig a new grave, a bit larger. Mother and daughter were placed beside each other in the little graveyard just north of the swamp, the graveyard for the slaves. No one commented on what had happened. And soon the earth was covered with a silent, white carpet.

The days rolled on and were as uninteresting as a blank sheet of paper. Reim worked and toiled from the moment daylight pierced through the opening in the roof in the morning until he threw himself, exhausted, down on the straw bedding in the evening.

Then one day, something happened.

Reim was on his way over to the farm's blacksmith to sharpen his knife. The skies were filled with flying snow flakes, and through the snow, he saw a boy, dressed in blue, out in the fields.

Reim gaped in astonishment. He had never seen the likes of this! The boy did not walk stamping up and down in the snow; he slid with his feet on top of the snow. When he came to a slope, he flew unbelievably fast. At the bottom of the hill, he rolled over and over in the snow. It looked so funny that Reim laughed out loud.

The boy was on his feet again. He brushed the snow off his clothes and lunged out across the pasture. Now Reim could see that he had long wooden boards fastened to his feet and it was these wooden boards that held him up.

"Wait!" Reim called. He wanted to try this for himself. But the boy was already too far away. He fairly flew towards the forest and disappeared into the snowstorm.

Una laughed when Reim questioned her in the yard. "That is nothing to get so excited about. You have just seen a boy out on skis, I should think!"

Reim felt no exhaustion that evening. He ran off with two of the boards the women used when they washed clothes, and sneaked outside. Then he stomped up to the forest grove. There was a hill there that was so steep, it seemed to descend into the centre of the earth. His stomach fluttered with excitement as he stood at the top and fastened the boards with sturdy ropes. Now, just to hold myself as stiff as a pin and close my eyes, he thought. And then he set off.

The next morning old Kumba exclaimed that the boy must have been attacked by evil spirits during the night. His face and hands were a mess of bloody cuts from somersaults in the hard, crusty snow.

Sometimes Tora came to the mill. She stood quietly waiting, in her ragged clothes, holding a goat on a leash. When no one was watching, Una quickly gave her a couple of handfuls of flour.

"Run down to Sigrid and her children with this bag, Reim," Una said one day. "It is hard enough to be a slave or a free farmer. Sigrid has no relatives in this area, and anyone who has no relations to help them is both poor and vulnerable."

When Reim hesitated, she quickly added, "Orm Viking is not here today, so you can go quite safely."

Reim fetched Tir, and they ran down the trail that led to the sea. The snow squeaked under their feet, and their breath crystallized into puffy, white clouds. Not far from the strand was a little, low hut that seemed to have rooted itself in the steep, rocky hillside. Just beside the hill a perpendicular rock wall jutted into the sky. Frosty smoke rose from the sea and drove as a rolling fog over the roof of the little cabin. Almost like a gopher's hole, Reim thought.

"By the god of thunder, is it both of you!" Tora's eyes widened at the sight of them. She pushed the warped door aside just enough to let them enter the hut. It took some time for their eyes to adjust to the darkness inside. A single lamp of rock cast a flickering reflection on the stone walls and on the glittering white frost covering the rafters. Three little boys crawled around on the floor playing with small wooden horses. Their ragged goat stood in the corner of the room, chomping on some dried moss. By the fireplace sat a meagre, little woman scraping a pot. Sigrid, Tora's mother, looked up and said, "Welcome to our farm! It has been some time, though, since we had a real farm." When they gave her the little bag of flour her eyes filled with tears. "May the goddess Froya reward Una for this."

Tora pushed a stool over to them. "Reim, you can sit on the high seat!" She stuck a splinter into the lamp's flame and sat down on her knees before the fireplace. "Now you will see, it will soon be warm here in the hall," she said shivering, as she huffed and puffed at the little fire that she had started. A sour smoke soon rose from the damp fir branches that had just been cut in the forest. Soon the fire crackled warmly, and Reim pushed his stool closer. His feet felt like frozen logs. He stretched his feet out towards the fire and first noticed that he was warm when he smelled the scorched leather.

Sigrid poured some water into a pot, adding dried nettles and a handful of flour.

And Tora slipped into her dream world, pretending that she was the wife of a great farm owner, waltzing around the room, setting a drinking horn full of mead on the table together with a tray of freshly baked bread. "Hurry now, servants," she called. "When are the silver dishes with baked birds, and where is the good wine?"

Her small brothers quickly joined her in this game. They hopped around, barking and wagging their rumps in the air, in an attempt to resemble trained dogs that were to show their tricks for these distinguished guests.

Sigrid poured the warm drink into a large bowl and sent it around. "We have such a long winter ahead of us," she sighed. "There is a time to sow, a time to reap, a time to eat, and a time to hunger. It has always been like this, and it seems that this is how the gods want to continue. Our only comfort is that after every winter, there comes a new spring, and a new summer...."

"Will you go to Iceland then?" asked Tir.

"To Iceland? No, well, no one can take your dreams from you, can they? I have heard that Iceland is such a beautiful land, with snow-decked mountains and green grassy fields. But it seems that those that draw to Iceland are the great folk who are looking for more lands for their sons. I do not think that anyone would want a poor widow on their slip."

At the end of the day Reim would often stop in at the cooking house to warm up. Vapour rose from the steaming pots.

"Is it you, Reim?" Kumba brushed a tangle of hair off her forehead and smothered the fire with a handful of ashes. "Come and sit down here beside me. What have you been up to today?"

Reim sulked. "I make some ropes and then I shovelled out the pig pen. I never do anything other than make ropes and shovel out the pig pen...." He stared at his hands. They were red and sore. "I do not want to slave any more, Kumba."

Kumba's face twisted into a wide grin. "Nobody wants to, boy. But even if you do not want to, you have to. No one is master of their own fate."

She got up and stirred the huge pot, and then sat down beside him again.

"Kumba, there is something I have been thinking about...."

Kumba winked at him with her small, black eyes. "Now then, let me hear what goes on in the back of that shiny red mane of yours."

"You make the food for the master's table, do you not?"

"Yes, I do. Sometimes Una helps me. I know that you are hungry, child, but it is difficult to napp food intended for the master's table."

"That is not what I wanted to say....." His eyes were fastened on the leather pouch that Kumba wore around her neck. He knew that she did not just have dried herbs in that pouch. She had the skin of an adder, the claws of an eagle, the paws of a wolf and some bones that she had dug from a grave mound on three Thursday nights under a full moon.

"Have you never thought of poisoning their food, Kumba?"

He had not known how Kumba would react, but he had not expected her to burst out in a howling laughter. She laughed so she nearly rocked right off the bench. How many times had children come to her with this proposition? And then she straightened up and looked at him angrily. "And who would get the blame if something like that happened? No one other that old Kumba, that is who. And I can also tell you that the earl and his wife have a slave taste all of their food before they dare eat it themselves. The old earl was poisoned, they say. He turned blue in the face and fell on the floor of the great hall. But no one believed the cook. She and three other slaves were hanged in that huge tree in the yard. They dingled there until the crows had taken care of them."

Reim sat, kicking the bench sulkily. "Have you ever been at the market, Kumba?"

"Yes, I sure have. When I was young. The earl wanted to talk with some beautiful young girls, ha, ha, ha.... Oh ya. There is quite a hustle and bustle there, I can tell you. There are merchants and craftsmen and ships from many lands. But the market place is a whole day's travel south of here."

"I want to escape and go to the market. Maybe Tir and I can get on board a ship that is on its way to Ireland." Kumba was furious now. "Hush!" she hissed. "Even the walls have ears around here. The earl has set out watches in the forest surrounding the farm. They have watch posts all over the place. Do you really think that a little slave boy like yourself is going to be able to trick them? You will be as easy to catch as a mouse in a trap. And the punishment will be much worse than you can imagine." Kumba rose and stirred the pot again. "The porridge is finished. The others will come some. Take ahold of the handle, Reim, and help me lift it down."

"And remember," she added. "I do not want to hear any more of this foolishness."

Evening in the slave quarters. Una raked the ashes and swung the heavy pot away from the hearth. Then she opened the door. "Huff! Icy wind out there." The snow whipped at her face and the wind took hold of her smock, blowing it up over her naked legs. She filled a bucket with snow and hurried in again. The snow sizzled as it hit the warm pot. The porridge had hardened on the bottom. She would have to scrape the pot in the morning.

She stood for a while looking at all the sleeping people. The fire was dying out, but she could still see the faces of the children piled up in the corner. The youngest of the Arabian girls had snuggled up beside her sister. She slept peacefully with her arm around a wooden doll. Beside them lay the two Irish children, cuddled tightly together. Their hair shone like copper in the faint gleam of light. Yrsa's little rascal was curled up like a kitten inside of his sheepskin bag. He was only two years old, too young to have bad dreams.

All of these children are slaves, thought Una. They are treated more like animals than people. They are the property of the earl and they have to work from early morning until late at night. Some of them had been stolen from their homes, and they could be sold at will at the market. They had absolutely no protection.

Strange the things these children say sometimes, she thought, smiling fondly to herself. Just the day before, little Muna had come to her and said, "You ought to have a great cart to push that big belly of yours around in, Una!" And Tir had laughed and said, "I remember when our cow at home in Ireland was going to have twin calves. Her stomach dragged on the ground and under that again she had great udders to drag around, too. At least you don't have to do that, Una!"

Una carefully laid a hand over her stomach. She could feel movement deep inside again. It felt just like the fluttering wings of a little bird. The first time she had felt this light, fragile movement she had been happy. Her own child! But after a while, she had become very depressed. Her child would be a slave, just as she, herself, and her parents had been. Her child would born to slavery, toiling for other people who were free!

And lately a new fear had worried her. What if she was not allowed to keep her child at all. This had been a poor year. There was little grain. And she saw their food supplies diminishing day by day. The earl would surely let her keep a boy child, because they became strong and capable men slaves. But a girl child would not be spared.... If she could just get near the marketplace, Una thought. There she had a relative, Bergliot. She was also of slave decent, but she was married to a free farmer. But the path to the market was closed. The earl's warriors kept watch day and night.

Una pulled her shawl tightly around her shoulders and laid down on the bed by the hearth. She had fallen into the habit of only sleeping for short periods of time. She had to watch that the fire did not go out. And she knew she had to get up when her back froze during the night.

⋯⋯⋯⋯⋯⋯⋯⋯⋯⋯⋯⋯⋯⋯⋯⋯

The winter sacrificial was nearing. Smoke rose from all the buildings on the farm that had fireplaces. The slave women bustled back and forth between the storage houses and cooking house, carrying large wooden troughs and tubs of meal between them. The men were busy brewing mead in one of the rock houses. The smells of baking and brewing filled the air.

One day, Reim mobilized all of his courage and slipped through the heavy oak doors of the temple where the sacrificial festivities were to take place. He stood in the middle of the room, his heart throbbing so hard he thought that his chest would burst. The pale light that slipped in through the smoke hole fell on a large stone altar, and in the darkness he could dimly distinguish the form of a ghastly face glaring at him with a sharp eye. That must be the god Odin, he concluded. The god who knows about everything that happens in the whole world and who had offered his one eye to the source of wisdom. He caught a glimpse of other terrifying faces in the dark. They were hewn into the log walls which, over the years, had turned black with soot. The vikings' gods! It was as if clammy hands were grasping for him. He ran, shivering, out of the dark hall, slamming the heavy oak door behind him.

New guests arrived daily, prepared to participate in the sacrificial festivities. When Reim pressed his eye up to a little hole in the pig pen wall, he could see the road from the north that wound into the yard through snow covered fir trees. Often he saw the glitter of silver and metal from harnesses and saddles in the dark forest, and then black, brown and fallow-coloured horses would trot at full speed out of the forest and into the farmyard. The ground rumbled and clouds of mist trailed after the warm horses. Some of the guests arrived on horseback and others drove in large sleds with their slaves and servants, their colourful clothing in extreme contrast to the white snow. Children were packed in wolf skin cloaks, and they squealed in delight when the horses sprinted the last distance. They lifted their arms and shook the huge iron rattles that they used while travelling to scare away wild animals and evil spirits on the trip.

There was much noise and commotion on the farm. Digralde and Vidur rushed back and forth, catching the horses by the reins as they galloped into the yard. On the stoop stood the earl and his wife. They were dressed in ankle-length blue smocks, abundantly decorated with silver and gold ornaments. The earl lifted his arms in greeting. His rumbling voice rose over the neighing, the tramping of the horses' feet, the laughter and calls of adults and children. "Welcome to this festivity, my kinsmen!"

A group of young boys sauntered across the yard. They were part of the group that had come to celebrate the winter sacrificial, and had decided to take a look around the farm.

Reim was ready to bolt the door for the evening and stood just for a moment in the door opening. He sensed that something was about to happen. He would have ducked out of sight but the boys had already seen him.

"And what have we here? A slave boy! Come, let's have a little fun!" The boys elbowed each other and laughed. They were dressed in red and blue coats and capes that were edged with fur. Some of them had swords or axes hanging from their belts. The largest boy was the leader. He was exactly what the people in this land thought a chieftain's son should look like; tall, well-built, with sharp blue eyes and hair as thick and golden as the mane of his fallow-coloured horse. He drew a knife from his belt and waved it under Reim's nose.

"Are you a muck digger, slave boy? Oh, and you can braid ropes! Maybe we should make a rope of your slave skin. That would be amusing!"

"Good idea, Narve," the other boys laughed.

Reim tried to worm his way against the back wall of the pig pen. The pigs whined and rolled away from him.

"Ha, ha, ha," the boys howled. "It's not possible to see which of the pigs are blackest in this bin. Come now, we can drag out the pig that is nearest!"

The boys grabbed Reim by the belt around his coat and lifted him out of the bin. One of the boys took him by the hair. "This one does not need a slave mark. He would have difficulty hiding with that blazing mane. What do you say, slave boy?" He pulled Reim's head back over.

Reim trembled. "I am not a slave," he sputtered. "I am Irish, and my father is a free farmer. He is a free man."

Narve laughed arrogantly. Reim felt his breath on his face. "You fool. I will have to show you who is master and who is slave!"

Reim felt a stinging blow in the stomach. Then a fist flew towards his face. Stars danced before his eyes and he fell to the ground, trying to protect his face with his hands. Between his spread fingers he could see the fists that were pounding him and the feet that were kicking him. Hard, harder, harder! He curled up in pain and rolled over, turning his face to the cold damp earth.

An ominous dark shadow fell across the door opening and into the room. The young boys shouted in fright and quickly disappeared, as if they had been scared by a monstrous ogre. They bounded across the yard to the banquet hall. And as far away as Reim was, he caught a glimpse of the warmth and light and gaiety inside. He saw the clowning buffoons dancing between the long beds of fire.

Reim lay still for a long time, his heart beating hard and quick against the cold earth. As he pulled himself up, he felt sick and had to throw up on a empty stomach.

"They did this to me because I am a slave." The thought hammered in his head. "Because I am different. Because I do not really belong here."

He held his head in his hands. Blood ran from the gash on his forehead and from his nose. The snow was covered with dark, bloody blotches. As he walked back to the slave quarters, he saw Digralde's immensely broad back ahead of him on the path. Digralde bowed his head under the door frame and disappeared into the low-ceilinged room. Reim followed him.

"What has happened to you?" Una whispered in fright when she saw Reim's face. When he did not answer her, she said, "I have saved a little of the porridge for you. Sit down in the corner and eat."

Old Klegge rolled over on his bed of hay. "Oh, but you smell like a pig, boy!" His laughter was a dry as the crackling of the log on the fireplace. "But then all slave boys smell of pig. I did too, when I was your age."

A new moon hung over the mountain, yellow and round like a bowl of freshly churned butter. "That is a good sign," said Kumba. "A full moon gives luck and fertility." The ancient slave woman rocked back and forth. Her eyes, barely visible through the snarled hair that hung across her face, sparkled. She mumbled, joining in the song that drifted across the yard to them from the temple. The sacrificial festivities had gone on all day long. The slaves had dragged goats and calves through the heavy oak doors, and finally they had led in the black horse that was to be offered on the stone alter. As the night fell, it was not difficult to hear that the mead was taking effect. The singing was often broken by noises: shouting and hysterical laughter.

The slaves leaned, half asleep, against the stone walls. Only the Irish children and old Kumba were wide awake. Why was Una gone such a long time, and where was Digralde? Tir crawled over to the slave woman and they sat quietly listening to the ancient songs. "Kumba," Tir asked. "Why do they sacrifice in this land?"

Kumba looked at her sharply. "Are you out of your mind, girl, to ask such a question? If we did not sacrifice, we would draw the wrath of the gods down upon us. The giant mountain in back of the farm would be torn into fragments, the skies would fall over us, and tongues of fire from the depths of the earth would consume us. The gods must have their offerings, do you understand? Blood and mead give strength. Strength to every living thing on this earth; to the grain that grows, to the animals and to the people themselves. If this is not true in the land you come from, how do the animals and people survive?"

Reim moved closer. "I saw a carving of Odin when I was in the temple," he whispered. "He looked frightening. Almost like the devil himself."

Kumba nodded, as she muttered, "The great Odin travels over land and strand on his swift horse, Sleipner. Two black ravens sit on his shoulder, spying at the world with sharp, cutting stares. Odin is ancient and wise, but cruel. He is the god of warriors. The earl and his viking warriors sacrifice to Odin."

"There were many other pictures of gods in the temple too."

"Oh, yes!" And now Kumba smiled, her eyes nearly disappearing under the many folds of skin.

"There are many gods to know. Froy, who sends the rain when the earth is thirsting, and the warmth of the sun to make the seeds sprout. His sister, Froya, helps men and women to have children, and the ox and cow to have calves!"

"And then there is Thor. Have you seen Thor when he rides his rams across threatening skies? Have you seen him when it thunder and lightning over yonder mountain tops? He lifts his hammer and strikes the air so sparks fly! Ya! Thor is a god that most people like. He is so enormously strong that he can cast evil spirits into stone. There are many trolls and evil spirits in the rocks on the steep mountain sides around here. If we did not have Tor, all of this evil would break loose around us all at once."

Tir shuddered. She was afraid of spirits and trolls. There were even more of them in this land than there were in Ireland. "What else can the gods do, Kumba?"

"Now you are asking too many questions, girl. They help in so many ways. I have already told you that the vikings pray to their gods for victory in war, and luck on their raids. But peaceful farmers pray for good years and peace."

Good years and peace. These were words he had heard before. Reim closed his eyes and leaned back against the wall. Suddenly it was as if it was Christmas and he was back home in Ireland. He could see his mother's face so clearly.

"Off you go now," she said. "And be sure to wash your ears and change into clean clothes." They combed the knots out of their hair and scrubbed themselves until their skin was hot and red. And they laughed as they put on their new clothes, because they felt so strange, as if they were not quite themselves any longer. And all of the people they met at the little monastery church acted strangely too. They looked so different in their fine clothes, their faces unusually solemn. The monk opened the golden latches on the calfskin book, and then he began to read the gospel. Candlelight reflected on his polished head and on the white lime-washed walls.

To start with, it was not difficult to stand still with folded hands. But after a while, he got such pains in his legs! The shadows on the wall grew long, and the monk's mouth reminded him of a mill, as in legend, that grinds and grinds for all eternity. The mass was in Latin, a foreign language that no one understood. His little sisters made faces and waved their braids to make him laugh. Mother's eyes looked at them sternly and she lifted a finger to her lips to keep still.

But when they had returned home again, she was Christmas-happy. She gave them each a cup of something strong and said, "Drink now, a Christmas toast! For a good year and for peace! So that we may have a good harvest and live in peace here in our land...."

Reim awoke abruptly from his daydream. Una stood in front of him, in the light from the hearth. They all laughed heartily when they saw her. "I think you are going to give birth to a troll baby, Una," Kumba said as she dried tears of laughter from her eyes, because this was certainly the largest stomach she had ever seen.

"And a troll baby it shall be." Una smiled mischievously as she drew forth a large leather bag she had hidden under her smock. The masters had finally gotten so drunk on the mead that she had been able to fill her bag. No one would dare criticize the changeling she had brought with her! She loosened the bands. The bag was full of warm horse meat.

The smell of fresh meat tingled the noses of the sleeping group surrounding them. They rubbed the sleep out of their eyes and gazed in wonder at the food Una had brought with her. A cheer rose when Digralde suddenly appeared in the room. He hit his head on the low rafters and swore nastily. But the young men quickly ran to his assistance and rescued the huge frothy bowl of mead he had just stolen from the cellar.

There was one person who was not at all amused: the monk. "This is sacrificial food!" he cried as he crossed himself. "No Christian can eat the meat of a horse!"

He sat scowling at them while they ate the meat. But the temptation was too great and he finally drew himself over to the last pieces. And he did not seem to mind the mead either, for after a while he joined into a frolicking dance with the slave girls in front of the crackling fire.

The room swayed, up and down. So strange. Reim sat with his mead bowl between his hands and laughed at Yrsa's little boy turning somersaults in the hay. Back in the furthest corner, he caught a glimpse of old Klegge, combing the lice out of his beard with a huge comb made of bone. "Got that one, ya. And that one!" he hummed in satisfaction and then stood up to show the others, only to fall back into the hay again. The mead made him happy for a few moments each year.

Then Yrsa shouted, "We can pray to Froya. Pray that she give Una a beautiful male child!"

They all assembled in a ring in front of the hearth. Kumba drew forth her leather pouch with magical herbs. She dumped some of the contents into a pot and started to chant. Blue and red tongues of fire licked at the pot. Kumba mumbled and sang, waving her arms over the grey-yellow steam that rose towards the ceiling.

> Wolves' claws and eagles' beaks
> Bright night and black day
> Dwarfs, gnomes, ogres, trolls
> Grant Una a fair young son.

Kumba's eyes shone like black stars over the edge of the pot. She asked Una to bend over the strong brew. Then she repeated the chant, and the others mumbled with her. Una's face glistened feverishly. She fell back on the bed of hay, and soon afterwards was sound asleep. One after the other, the slaves found an empty place on the floor. They tumbled over each other and rolled in the straw.

Reim had to run outside for a very necessary errand, but his legs were not very steady. As he sent a fine stream down the walls of the house, it seemed as if the moon was laughing at him, way up there on the edge of heaven.

As long as the winter sacrificial continued, Reim hid in the furthest corner of the horses' stall. He watched through a hole in the wall until the last guest had left the yard by horse and sled, with much noise and commotion.

"Is this where you have been hiding?" Reim felt a heavy hand on his shoulder and jumped. "I did not mean to scare you, boy!" Digralde's clear blue eyes smiled. "No one knows better than I do what it is like to get beaten up by the master's young whelps. I was made a slave when I was just six winters old."

Digralde stared straight ahead. It was as if he was talking to himself. "When I have a nightmare, do you know what I see? I see a boy, led by his father's large, secure hand. They walk together up to the high seat. There the man lets go of the little hand to receive something glittering. 'Father, what are you doing?' the little boy calls. The father turns to leave. 'Father, where are you going Father? Father, Father answer me!' But a father's back holds no answers. And the earl's warriors grab the little boy."

The winter was long. As the grey daylight sifted in through the skin that covered the smoke hole, Reim crept out of his sheep skin and pulled on his padded tunic. He always slept fully clothed for two reasons: the straw stuck him in the back, and it was so cold in the stone hut that he could see his own breath—white clouds puffing in front of his face. It took him some time to get ready to go out in the wet, biting snow. He had frost sores on his legs, and therefore had to wind long strips of rags around them. First one layer of rags, and then a layer of straw, and then more rags. When he was finally finished, his legs resembled stiff logs from the knee down.

The winter seemed never ending. The people on the farms hungered and starved, and on the roads roamed many beggars and children pleading for food. The nights could be terrifying. Long, drawn out howls from the wolves that were nearing the farms sounded in the darkness.

Hunger guested the earl's farm also. The slaves felt it most. Reim was pained at seeing Tir's thin, pale face as she sat bent over her food bowl. The girls were always given the least. Every day he promised himself that he would give her some of his own food. But every single day he devoured his food and scraped up every last bit in his bowl.

And then one day something happened that they all had feared. Digralde came into the slave quarters and slammed his fist into the door frame.

"What in the world is the matter with you," Klegge wondered. "It looks as if you have slain a bear and have not received your due for the skin!"

"Save your jokes for some other time," Digralde said sullenly. "I was just informed that eight slaves will be sold to a chieftain from the grain area."

Silence resounded in the little house. Everyone looked at each other. Thirty slaves sat there. Thirty slaves that had lived and worked together for a long, long time. They had fought and sworn at each other; they had begrudged each other's food and warm beds. Now all of this was forgotten.

Reim stood close to Tir and could feel her despair seeping right through her clothes. They both thought the same thing: they might never see each other again. Yrsa's little boy crawled around on the floor playing with a wooden horse. His mother picked him up and cuddled him tightly.

The chieftain from the grain district was a short, stout man with an enormous stomach. He did not look as if he had hungered at all this hard winter. He sat by a table, fattening himself on grouse and reindeer meat, which the slave girls carried to him on large silver platters. This type of food was seldom eaten on the flatland farms where he lived.

He bent forward, sorting through the flock of slaves. "Where is that giant of a slave of yours, Earl? The one that lifted my sacks of grain as if they were down-filled pillows!"

The earl laughed and filled a horn with mead for his guest. "The slave you mentioned will not be sold, not even if you offer me four of your finest horses. He is going to be with me on the viking raids this summer."

The earl walked across the floor and pulled the English monk out of the group. "Here is a slave that is just as good. He just might talk you to death, though, about the weak god that folk on the other side of the sea believe in. But you can always place him with your buffoons!"

The chieftain smacked his lips as he gnawed on a leg of reindeer meat. He scrutinized the monk with eyes that were mere slits. "Ya, ya. Possibly not such a bad deal." He picked out four other men whom he thought looked healthy and strong. Leggjalde was one of them.

And then he noticed the two dark-skinned girls. "There are two beautiful young ladies," he said as he licked his lips. "I can always find something for them to do on my farm." Suddenly he pointed at Tir. "And I will take the red-headed girl also."

Reim saw Tir collapse. She seemed to shrink until she looked very little in her wide smock. Her shoulders started to tremble.

Then the earl's wife broke in, "You will have to get along with just the two dark-skinned girls, dear kinsman. I have already made other plans for the girl with the red hair. She is mine."

The chieftain pouted. He wiped the fat off his face with the back of his hand. "Never have I been any place where it has been so difficult to buy slaves. If you were not my kinswoman, dear Gudrun, I would just return home with my load of grain. Then you would really feel the bite of hunger on this farm." He grunted in dissatisfaction and pointed at Yrsa.

Yrsa shrieked like a dog that had been beaten. "I will go nowhere without my child. He is the son of the earl!"

"Quiet, woman," hissed the earl. And Orm Viking moved quickly to her side and gave her a blow across the back.

The earl's wife addressed the chieftain. She smiled sweetly. "You can have the slave whelp on top of the bargain, dear kinsman."

"And feed him for ten years before he is worth anything," snorted the chieftain. "If justice was to be done here, I should only pay half price for a slave woman who drags along a child."

"Yrsa is a clever slave woman and knows more than most about the work on a farm." The earl's wife straightened. "You need just such a woman, now that your wife has left you and has gone home to her father's farm.

The chieftain's face grew dark. But then he threw his head back and laughed heartily. No one knew if it was the flippant answer of his kinsman's wife, or the mead that had loosened his laughter belt. He toasted with the earl. It finally looked as if both were satisfied.

"Get going!" Orm Viking kicked the nearest slave to start them all running across the yard.

The slaves packed what few things they owned into a bundle: a wooden bowl, a couple of wooden spoons and a bent piece of iron that was used to strike against flint, creating sparks to start a fire. Yrsa's dear little light-haired boy ran to them all, giving out hugs before tightly clutching his mother's smock and disappearing through the door. Many of the slaves stood with tears in their eyes as they watched him.

Muna rustled quietly over to Tir. She stared at the floor as she said, "Take care of this for me, will you? I am sure we will meet again." And then she pressed her wooden doll into Tir's arms.

Within a short time, the chieftain had gathered his people. The slaves were to walk in the back, after the last wagons and horses. They were tied with ropes.

The ropes that I braided, Reim thought. He stood watching the train of slaves until the last one disappeared into the darkness of the great fir forest.

One bitterly cold winter day, Tir and Reim were sent out to gather moss to feed the animals.

"If you walk towards the river, you cannot go wrong," Kumba said. They followed the hard, trampled path that weaved like a thin, blue ribbon through the new snow. Here and there were tracks left by men who had gone hunting in the woods on skis, following the path through the woods up to the mountains. When they reached the narrow wooden bridge that crossed the river, a little sod pile appeared before them. They loosened the stiffly frozen pieces of moss and tied them together to secure a load.

They had a fine time together while they were working. They laughed and talked. Tir told Reim that she had seen the earl's son again. The warriors had taken him out in the fields to practise riding and the use of weapons.

"I just hope he stays far away from me," Reim commented. "I have seen enough of these rich men's sons."

By the time they lifted the great loads of moss onto their backs, the shadows in the forest had already grown long. The wind whistled over the mountain ridge in the north.

"We had better start back," Reim said. He drew Tir with him through the thickest part of the forest. "I am sure we came this way."

They walked and walked and could not find the path back to the farm. They stopped, frightened and out of breath. There was no other way out. They had to turn around and go back to the bridge, then follow the river down to the valley. The river bustled, a wide, green hollow cutting deeply into the white snowy earth. Like sharp spears of glass, icicles hung over the rock-strewn slope. Under the ice, water gurgled and roared, like the rumbling of troll voices.

Suddenly they heard a long howl far, far away. Was it the wind blowing through the trees, or the sound of the waterfalls? They froze and stood listening intensely.

"It could be wolves," Tir said, her face pale in the dim light. Reim shuddered. He imagined the sharp teeth and the red, ravenous jaws. He grabbed Tir's hand.

Then they heard the howl again, a long, drawn-out lamenting wail. It could be some evil spirit, one that they would not dare mention by name, Reim thought. Goose bumps ran down his back. The pack of troll spirits that would lure them into a grave mound, or change them into stone!

They stood there, not knowing what to do, looking at each other, feeling terror take hold of them, their hearts throbbing out to their fingertips. But when the wailing started again, they waded right through the snow in the direction the sound was coming from. It had to be a person; only a person could shriek like that!

Tir cried a shout of relief as she reached the edge of the forest. Now she knew where she was. Right under them was the level land that they called the washing area. The slave women washed the clothes there in the whirling cold river water and, during the winter, fetched water there.

Tir thought she could see something moving by the water's edge. They slid down the hill, with their loads still on their backs.

"Is anyone here?" they called, their hearts pounding in their throats.

"Froya be praised," a voice answered. It was Una's voice. She had fallen in the snow, and her water buckets were floating away, down the swirling river. "Help me," she cried. "I have to get into the hut."

They had to hurry. They supported Una between them. She leaned heavily as she groped through the deep snow. Her hands were frozen blue. She bit her lips and moaned softly, clutching tightly at her stomach.

They crossed the bridge that spanned the river's mouth and reached the safety of the mill. Reim ran the shortest path to Kumba. "You have to come. Una has fainted in the mill!"

Kumba quickly grabbed a pot of boiling water and took the other slave women with her. As she ran down the crooked path, she chided loudly, "Foolish slave girl. Going down to the river, now, when she is so great with child that she could stumble over her own stomach!"

When the women arrived, Tir and Reim crept out of the room and into the little lean-to. They sat with their ears to the wall. They heard Una shriek, and Kumba started chanting her runes. She called on the three Scandinavian norns that control the destiny of every newborn child, and she called on Froya and every god that she could think of who could help.

I carve the runes. The runes of birth.
The runes of birth for the son of a slave....

Tir and Reim recited the *pater noster* and other verses in Latin, which they could remember from their church back home in Ireland. They did not know what they meant, but they hoped that they would be of some help. Their neighbour's wife had died in childbirth. Heaven help poor Una....

They heard steps on the frozen path. Terror struck their hearts as they recognized the rat-like form of the slave driver in the door opening, and they crawled further back into the corner of the lean-to. He held a stick in his hand.

"What is going on here," he growled. "Not one single slave woman at the farm when the earl receives guests!" He hit the nearest slave woman across the back, and swore, "For the sake of great Odin, women! Get up to the hall!"

But then he stopped. In the middle of the flock of women he saw Una's tortured face. He swore again and quickly walked away.

A short while later, they heard the slight but angry cry from a vital new life.

"I am so happy," Tir whispered as she dried her eyes.

Reim laid his ear to the wall. "No one seems to be very happy in there," he said shortly. Kumba is cursing all of the gods in Valhalla, and Una is crying. They said it was a girl."

They received instructions from the earl's hall that the newborn girl was to be set out for the wolves. "Slave women reproduce faster than the pigs," the earl commented curtly. "The only difference is that a pig grows up faster. Slave children have to be fed at least ten years before they are worth their food."

Digralde's eyes darkened when he heard this. He lifted his child in his arms. "Your name was to be Astrid," he said so softly that only the slaves sitting nearest heard him. They wondered. Astrid was no slave name. Then the father packed the child in sheepskins and disappeared out into the frigid winter night.

The slaves sat silent. They had gone through this many times before. It was common for slave children to be laid out in the forest to die. Only Una wept loudly, mournfully, on her bed.

At midnight Digralde tramped back into the room. "Quiet now, woman," he growled when he heard Una's wailing. "If you do not stop that crying, no one will have any peace in this room!" But then he walked over to her and whispered softly that he had taken the little bundle down to Sigrid's sod hut. The poor widow had shouted in complaint when she saw Digralde's errand. If she was to have even more to struggle with, they would surely all starve to death. She told him to use his common sense. He was a slave.

But Digralde had both threatened and begged. He would manage to provide food somehow, even though he knew that the punishment for thievery was severe. They beat the men slaves, and if a woman slave stole, they cut off one of her ears. But that was a risk they would have to take.

"Give our little Astrid a chance," he begged. "Give her the chance to live just one day at a time."

And finally, Sigrid relented. She took the little bundle in her arms, and before she could change her mind, Digralde was out of the door.

Three days later, another girl child was born at the farm. She was the daughter of the earl. There was almost as much activity tied to this event as there was to the winter sacrificial. Women from the large farms in the area came with gifts and presents. The earl's wife was thrilled that Una had just given birth. Her breasts were full of milk and she could nurse their little daughter.

And so one day, winter was over. The snow crept up the steep hills and the thin, pale blue air was filled with sunshine. Coltsfoot thrust their tasselled yellow heads up out of the clay, and the river flowed, foaming, white and frothy, down the mountainside, singing, spring is here!

At this time of year, the vikings readied their ships. As soon as the bay was free of ice and shining blue, they could set forth. These were busy days at the larger farms and at the farms of the chieftains. The slaves readied troughs of bread, boxes of salt meat and dried fish, and barrels of fresh water. It took them many days to drag and carry the supplies on board the low, wide ships that smelled of new tar. On the strand, grey smoke rose from the smithy's. The district's smithy stood in front of the glowing forge, his face as black as the earthen floor he stood upon. He sharpened the battle axes, swords and spears, and he beat out new arrow-heads—sharp weapons to use on human flesh, they all knew.

Altogether, twelve ships were to leave this time. The boat builders inspected every inch of the ships, both inside and out. The earl had also had a new ship built. There was room enough in it for fifty men at the oars, and the prow was decorated with a golden vane. The earl called the ship *Dragon*. With this ship, he planned on sailing to the Orkney Islands, where he had kinsmen, and then sailing to the south and plundering the Irish seas.

"See the black ravens that circle around the ship up there," whispered Kumba. "They are a sign of death and tragedy for those that are visited by these ships during the coming summer."

"Many never return from these journeys," Una cried as she thrust herself into Digralde's arms.

Digralde did not answer. He turned quickly away from her, diverting his attention to the activity of the other men down by the ship.

Reim spied around the field that he was hoeing with the other slaves. The tall figure of Orm Viking was not in sight. He sneaked quickly in back of a cluster of juniper bushes and continued climbing up a knoll until he could see out over the bay.

He reached the top just in time to see the viking ships start out. He heard the shouts of the oarsmen, and saw the sunlight reflecting on their oar blades as ship after ship left the bay area. Women, children and the elderly stood on the strand, waving and calling until they could no longer see the men on board. Small children whimpered, "Father, Father."

At the mouth of the bay new ships joined them. They came from the inlets and straits along the bay arm. Quite suddenly the group of ships had grown to a great naval force. The wind blew briskly out at sea. Their huge square sails folded out, and the ships sailed like a great flock of black birds, out of the lee.

Reim filled his lungs with the spring air. He shuddered to think of the vikings' mission. But it was amazing how quickly all of these dark thoughts vanished with the shining sun, heating up the earth beneath his bare feet.

On his way back to the farm, Reim spotted a light haired boy dashing between the hardwood trees on the south side of the yard. The boy was quick on his feet, and scampered like a chipmunk between the tree trunks as he spied up towards the tops of the trees. Suddenly he stopped. Not a muscle moved. In a flash he raised his bow and shot. The arrow flew through the branches and leaves right to the top of the tree. A deathly cry filled the air, the flapping of a bird's wings, and then the bird fell to the earth, glistening blue-black.

"Hurrah!" Reim shouted. This reminded him of his good days back in Ireland, when he was free and could run like the deer through the forest with Brian and practice archery. He completely forgot that he should have kept hidden in back of the hazel bushes. He burst forth shouting in excitement, "That was quite a shot!"

The boy turned around slowly and looked at Reim, starting at his dirty feet bound in rags up to his lice bitten face under such fiery red hair.

"I always hit my mark," he said, and the words were as sharp as the arrow he had shot through the air. He crossed his arms over his chest and planted his foot firmly on top of the bird laying dead on the ground.

"And I swim faster than the fish in the water. I can ride faster on my colt, Fakse, faster than Odin himself on Sleipner. I am as sure a shot as the goddess of hunting, Skade. And I can carve the secret runes. The son of an earl must be able to do all of these things."

Reim stood speechless, listening to this torrent of words. Such an arrogant fool really deserves a sound thrashing, he thought. But the memory of his own ill treatment by the sons of these great men was too fresh. So he held his temper, and instead said, "And I am Irish, and I too know how to bend a bow. Come, I will show you!"

Before the earl's son had time to protest, Reim had grabbed his bow. He placed the head of the arrow between his forefinger and his middle finger, and tightened the bow. "Can you see that bird way up there?" he said, pointing towards a little black speck high up in the vault of the heavens.

A swish with his bow, and the arrow flew through the air, higher and higher towards the target. And bull's-eye! Seconds later a large game bird fell right at their feet.

Reim jumped in joy. Una would be happy now. Such a fine, fat bird was a delicacy to cook into soup. But then he quieted. Now I have done something wrong again, he thought. A slave should not show an earl's son that he can shoot with a bow and arrow. Reim pulled the arrow out of the dead bird and gave the bow back to its rightful owner.

To his surprise, he saw that the fair-haired boy was smiling! He really looked quite comical because he had just lost two corner teeth. That made him seem much less pompous and honourable. He looked very simply like a young boy with quick eyes and tousled hair.

"I did not know that slaves could handle a bow that well!" He nodded in acknowledgement. "Should we have a duel out in the pasture in the middle of the forest?"

Reim completely forgot the work he was supposed to be doing as he followed the boy's blue back, down the soft mossy path that led into the forest. It smelled wonderful there. Under the tree trunks, the forest floor was covered with shimmering white and light green anemone.

The earl's son bent back some branches and stopped just before entering a little, green pasture. Exactly in the middle of the field grew an ancient, knotted oak tree with a mighty trunk and branches that extended high up into the heavens. There they tried to target shoot. They laughed and ran until they were warm and sweat, retrieving their fallen arrows under the tree trunk.

Suddenly the sky started dripping and trickling into the spring grass. "Come, we can sit in the secret hole," the earl's son said. He drew Reim with him into the hollow oak tree. They huddled close together, listening to the rain outside.

"By the way, my name is Sigurd," the earl's son said, as he scratched a mosquito bite on his leg.

"Sigurd? What a strange name!"

"I was named after Sigurd Fåvnesbane. Have you really never heard that legend?"

Sigurd looked at Reim very secretively, and then he pulled something out from the lining of his cloak. It was a small wooden figure that he had carved all by himself. It looked like a dragon with gaping jaws, and was such a fine piece of work that Reim would not have been surprised if it had leapt out of his hands into the grass, spitting tongues of fire at them.

"Once there was a dragon that guarded a great treasure," said Sigurd. "The dragon's name was Favne and no one dared come near the monster. No one besides our hero, Sigurd. He went to a blacksmith and had the smithy forge a sword that had a sharper blade than any other weapon in the land. Sigurd held his sword high in the air as he rode off to the dragon's cave. The dragon stuck his head out of the cave, breathing and spitting fire and sulphurous vapours. But Sigurd was not afraid of anything. He charged the dragon and stuck his sword right through the giant monster. and then he rode away with the tremendous golden treasure."

"That is what my father wants me to be like," Sigurd said. "Like the brave dragon killer!" Reim shuddered. It was scary to think of the ferocious dragon Sigurd told of. He sat for a while and wiggled a loose tooth, wondering if he did not have something just as exciting to tell Sigurd about. And then he said, "The man that I am named after was Irish and his name was Saint Patric. He lives up in heaven some place. St. Patric fights alongside of God and all his angels, against the devil and his warriors. They fight like cats and dogs, every single day. The devil has a huge and frightening army, and they cause chaos wherever they ride on their war horses. It is not easy to capture an angel, because they have wings and can fly away. And then God comes and throws rays of light at the devil's army, and they fall head over heels off their horses."

"That God must be just as strong as Odin," Sigurd said thoughtfully.

It stopped raining. Sigurd crawled out of the tree trunk and threaded his arm through his bow. "Now I have to go." He straightened up. "I have so many other more important things to do, slave boy."

As Reim ran back to his filthy place of work that day, he was happier than he had been since leaving Ireland.

Una knew what had to be done to keep her little daughter alive. But one day everything went wrong.

She slinked quickly across the dew-damp grass in the meadow. Far away in the green she could hear the grasshoppers playing their fiddles. Otherwise it was quiet, completely quiet. The moon threw a pale light over Stygg mountain and the trees cast long shadows.

A watchman sat just outside of the storage house as usual. He nodded, half asleep, his shield covering half of his face. His sword and spears lay on the ground beside him.

Suddenly, with a shriek, a crow flew up from a nearby tree, and flapped loudly with its blue-black wings. The guard grabbed his sword and Una fell flat on her stomach in the grass. She lay completely still until the guard fell asleep once again.

Una did not lose her composure. She dragged her smock up over her legs and tied it securely with a rope. Then she ran around to the back side of the storage house, where solid log walls stood in the dark shadows.

As agile as a weasel, she scaled the log walls. Digging her nails into the wood, she dragged herself over to the opening gaping towards her like a dark mouth just under the eves of the house. She was thankful that she had such strong arms. She grabbed a hold of the frame and pulled herself through. Had she been discovered? She heard steps on the gravel just below. Probably just one of the guards on a very necessary errand. She heard a splash and a trickle down the walls of the house. Then the guard slouched back to the others. Una let her breath out again.

She was in the loft. Little by little, her eyes adjusted to the dark. Just under the rafters hung row upon row of hams and dried meats. Along the walls were flour sacks and wooden pans with cheese and butter. Una stuck her finger into the soft butter and tasted it. Nothing in the wide world tasted as good as butter. And that was something the slaves had to do without.

She had to hurry. Quickly, she withdrew the knife she had hidden in the lining of her smock. Then she pulled a stool out onto the floor and climbed upon it, balancing on her toes, to cut down some of the dried meat. She did not dare take a ham.

Waves of shock flew through her as she felt something soft and furry climb up her leg. She let out a little cry, and fell at the same time, pulling a ham with her in the fall. A little, frightened mouse scampered between the flour sacks and then disappeared into the darkness.

She heard heavy tramping on the steps, and just seconds later she was caught. She stared into the evil face of Orm Viking. He held a torch in front of him and his eyes blazed at her like two black rocks in the gleam of the fire. "Seems that not only mice scuttle around here in the dark of night." He sneered and kicked her to make her get up. Una felt her heart fly up to her throat. Fear made it impossible for her to breathe.

Orm Viking grabbed her thick, curly hair. And then he laughed hoarsely, and whispered close to her cheek, "Wonder what you will look like without those fine ears of yours, woman. Many a fine slave woman has lost her beauty because of such a hankering for food that is meant for the master's table!" He grabbed her ear and slashed. Una felt a hot pain jogging through her head. A thick, red stream of blood trickled down her neck and dripped onto her smock.

The warriors were totally bored with having to sit guard night after night, just staring out into the darkness. So they did not let poor Una go until they tired of this welcome diversion. Then they threw her down the steps and let her creep back to the slave quarters.

Just a short time later, Tir was summoned into the hall to the earl's wife.

Tir remembered all too clearly the words that were said the first day she stood in the hall. "I am sure I will have use for this lively girl. I will remember her when the time comes...." Unruly butterflies fluttered deep down in her stomach. A cold sweat broke out on her forehead and hands.

The earl's wife lay in bed, propped up by pillows and fur rugs. She held two small dogs in her arms, petting them. Her fair-haired son sat by the hearth, whittling on a piece of wood. An elderly woman servant rocked a cradle. The baby in the cradle cried and waved her small arms.

"See Orm Viking to find a new slave that can nurse my child," the earl's wife said to the servant. "Una will not do any longer. When a slave loses an ear, she loses her milk also!"

Then she turned her attention to Tir. "Come a little closer," she coaxed.

Tir walked slowly across the floor. The earl's wife spoke softly. "And what is it you have around your neck, child?"

"It is a cross." Tir showed her the little cross her father had cut out of wood.

"I have heard about this Christian faith. The earl tells of your peculiar houses of worship, bulging with precious treasures. I would like to see one of these places with my own eyes. But we women seldom travel out into the world."

Tir told her that in the monasteries men and women praised and prayed to their God.

"But one cannot live by just praising this God alone." The earl's wife laughed.

"They have a huge garden. They grow vegetables and fruit. And they have a stable with goats and cows and sheep."

"Do they never go on raids then?"

Tir thought a bit. She had heard her father tell of some of the church's men who were evil and greedy, that had gathered many riches just for themselves. But then she only knew the good-natured Brother Cormac and the old village priest. She said, "The monks have taught us that we shall not kill, nor steal, and that we should not be evil towards one another. But we are not good at keeping these commandments."

The earl's wife looked at her thoughtfully. And then she straightened up and smiled. "Now I will tell you why I called you here. Go over to the cradle and tell me what you think of the little one lying there."

Tir walked across the floor and looked down into the cradle. Among silk feather bedding and embroidered blankets, she saw an angry little baby that most of all resembled one of the pink piglets that Reim took care of in the pig pen.

"Isn't she just beautiful," the earl's wife said. Her eyes gazed down at the child fondly. "All three of my oldest children died at the edge of a sword. They are now in Odin's kingdom. I just have Sigurd and this little child left. Froya be praised that it was a girl. She will not go out on viking raids."

"The earl's wife has thought to bestow upon you a great honour," the servant woman whispered. "Soon you will understand why. Watch the child when she cries."

Tir bowed over the baby in the cradle. As she opened her mouth in a loud bawl a little tooth came into sight. It was not any larger than a barley corn.

The earl's wife came over to her "My daughter should have a present on a great day such as this. You are to be her tooth present!"

Tir stared at her. A living person as a present!

The servant woman winked at her and continued in a whispering tone. "Tomorrow you will be moved into the great house instead of having to live in the draughty corner of the slave quarters. You will be given a hot bath to be sure you are rid of any lice. And there you will be given new clothes."

A tooth present! Angry tears gushed from her eyes. She was now owned by that little, red, screaming bundle lying in the cradle. She had been given away as if she was a calf at the market place. She turned towards the door.

"Wait! Just one moment," the earl's wife called after her. She loosened something from her smock and handed it to Tir. It was a little silver gilted brooch with an Irish pattern.

"I thought perhaps you would like to have this," the earl's wife said, looking almost shameful. A pale blush flushed across her face.

And then came summer.

The fields flowered. The wind rustled through wild chervil and dandelions, daisies and bluebells. Tir ran in the fields and picked strawberries that she threaded onto a straw. Every once in a while she put a strawberry into the mouth of the little girl sitting in the grass, stretching her arms out of her.

They had good days now. Una, Kumba and some of the slave women had moved up to the mountain dairy farm with the animals. There they made cheese and churned butter and did not return to the farm until the fall. Tir had to stay at the farm. The earl's wife soon noticed that Tir had a very good way with her child.

"You cannot have any more," Tir said firmly, when little Kjellaug cried for more berries. "You will hurt your stomach, so just keep quiet now!"

The little girl fell silent. Tir lifted her up and carried her over to Tora. She was holding a dappled cow by a rope, waiting for it to be finished chomping on the sweet clover that grew by the river banks.

"Come, we can climb up the hill."

They arrived, sweaty and out of breath, at the mountain ridge where Reim was watching a flock of sheep. He had driven the animals onto a luxuriant grazing land between a rock cliff that stretched up on one side, and a fence of solid poles on the other, which stopped the animals from wandering any further. As long as the animals stayed behind fence Reim could lay in the grass, chewing on a straw and staring into the blue summer skies where larks twittered happily!

"You lazy bones!" Tir and Tora said simultaneously.

Tir carefully set the earl's daughter down in the grass and Tora tied her cow to the trunk of a maple tree. "Shall we play the same game as yesterday?"

Tir did not wait for an answer, but started gathering twigs and cones. Tora ran quickly to a place where there was thick, green moss. She filled her lap and then carried the load carefully over to the ridge.

"I get to be the earl, like we did yesterday," Reim said.

"And I am a chieftain," Tora said.

They positioned the cone-cows into row upon row. They were gleaming red and shining in the summer sun.

"Tir, you can be a slave," the other two teased, "because you are the youngest. No cows for you, Tir!"

Tir showed them her fists in anger. "Then I do not think that I want to play any more!" She kicked the cone-cows so they flew over the edge of the mountain ridge.

"Well, then you can be the king. And you can have ten cows more than we have!"

Tir agreed to that. They played king, earl and chieftain, and none of them owned less than thirty cows. The cows stood in small stables made of sticks and rocks, with pieces of moss on the top.

And then Tir decided that she could trade ten of the strawberries that she had on her straw for ten shining cone-cows. The earl was tempted. They counted out the cows and exchanged. The chieftain licked her lips. She was not difficult to persuade either. The berries were juicy and dark red; they tasted of summer.

Tir ended up with all of the live stock, more than one hundred cone-cows. "Now, I am the greatest king of all!" she laughed, satisfied. "And you two are rightfully my slaves, without as much as an old cow skin to your names!"

They heard a call coming from down in the valley. Tora's cow had to go home to be milked. Tir lifted her little burden. She had fallen asleep in the soft grass.

"Who is running down there?" asked Tora.

"Where?" Tir searched until she saw a blue figure disappearing into the leaves of the forest.

"That must be Sigurd. Do you think that he has been sitting up on the ridge spying on us?" Tora shrugged. "Must be boring to be the son of an earl."

The girls started on their trip down the mountain side. "Be sure not to fall asleep again, Reim," Tir teased. "It is soon evening."

He must have slept a long, long time, because when he woke up the sun threw long shadows across the pasture. He stretched and sighed contentedly.

Then he jumped up and rubbed his eyes. Was this a bad dream? The fence that he had set up for the animals had been torn down. Not one single sheep could be seen.

Reim felt a prickling fear working its way down his back. Where should he look? There were paths all over the place out here. Some of them went towards the east over to the neighbouring district, and other paths climbed higher and higher up to the summer dairy farms in the mountains. It was most likely that the animals had gone towards the luscious pastures up on the mountains.

He started running between the heather and blueberry bushes, his heart beating wildly. He had to go through the birch forest and go near Stygg mountain in the north. He stopped a couple of times to wipe sweat off his face with his jacket arm. And then he ran on.

A figure suddenly appeared on the path before him, a burly man dressed in a brown jacket, the hood pulled down over his face. In his hand he held a bear spear.

Reim jumped out of his way. But the man stopped, broad-legged, right in front of him on the path and blocked his way. "Don't be frightened, lad," he growled. "I an no wayfaring tramp, if that is what you are afraid of." The man pulled back his hood, and Reim saw a pair of twinkling eyes gazing at him good-naturedly. The grey-bearded face said, "What is a little lad like yourself doing out here so late at night? There are bears and wolves in this area. Even a slave values his life, so it is best you turn around and start back, before the black of night."

Reim had not expected such friendly words from a stranger. And without really knowing what he was doing, a whole stream of words flowed out of his mouth, between frightened hiccups. Salt tears rolled down his cheeks and into the corners of his mouth as he told the stranger of everything that had happened.

The man scratched his beard. "Well, if that is how it is, then I guess that Farmer Brede will have to follow you a ways. I saw some sheep just under a cliff at Stygg mountain. There were also lambs in the flock. I thought they belonged to the Ullin's summer dairy farm up in the mountains, and did not give it any more thought."

"That must be my sheep," Reim shouted happily. He followed the farmer up the rocky slope. He felt safe as he followed this broad back. Farmer Brede's bear spear shone like a lance in the shimmering light. Reim sweated to think that he had run over these woodless upland without as much as a sharp pole or a rock sling to protect himself. He thought he heard sounds everywhere now. Probably just some small animal out on a nightly round, he thought. Maybe a weasel or a marten. Or maybe? Brede stopped and listened. From the plateau in the west came a long, drawn-out howl. "Wolves," he said shortly. "But they are far, far away."

Reim stopped and picked up a rock to carry in his hand. He followed Brede closely, constantly turning around to keep an eye on the path behind them.

The skies faded in the south, and the moon came up. The mountain enclosures shone nearly white in the night light. Right in front of them rose Stygg mountain, drifting clouds floating around the top. At the foot of this mountain Brede had seen the missing sheep. He started to walk faster, and Reim ran closely behind him, sweat beading on his forehead. They waded through the heather and tall ferns. Brede kept watch to all sides. Suddenly he saw something light in the tall grass. He let out a sharp cry. It was a lamb. The white wool was saturated with blood.

"Mighty forces have been at work here!" Brede said, pursing his lips. "We are wisest to wait and come back during the day. I can take a couple of men with me then. "

Reim nodded silently. He knew that Brede was right. But he had tears in his eyes. He could see the rest of the flock of sheep now. They were gathered under the mountain ridge, the small lambs pressed closely into their mothers.

As Brede turned to start down the path, something happened. Suddenly they heard a deep growl and a monstrous, dark shadow vaulted out of the scrub. The small lambs bleated in terror. Moments later the full-grown bear had taken his prey. The bear bounded off with the carcass of a sheep, right towards Reim and Brede!

"I'll stop you, you killer!" Reim shrieked. He threw the rock he had in his hand. It swished through the air and hit, with a crack, the skull of the huge, furry animal.

"Are you mad, boy!" Brede said, backing away and grabbing his spear. The animal immediately noticed the two creatures half hidden in the scrub and turned and bounded towards them, crushing branches and twigs beneath him.

Reim bent down in a flash and picked up a new rock, but this time he missed. The rock hit the mountain wall. The bear rose up on his back legs, furious.

And then Reim saw something he would never be able to forget. Just as the raging animal was about to throw himself over his prey, Brede planted his spear hard into the ground and quickly drew back. The heavy animal stood swaying for a long, long moment before throwing himself down onto the ground. The sturdy spear penetrated the bear, all the way to its heart.

Brede sank down on his knees. "This type of hunting could be the end of an old man," he said as he dried the sweat from his brow. And then he growled angrily, "You must be out of your mind, boy, provoking the king of the forest like that!"

Reim walked around and saw the results of the bear's visit. Dead sheep were spread all around, mostly lambs.

"We had better start back to the valley again," Brede said after a while. "My wife, Bergliot, will be worried by now." He grinned broadly. "She probably thinks that I have been attacked by a bear!"

Reim gathered the sheep and drove the frightened flock in front of him, down the path. The sky was pitch black, but down in the valley, torches on the house walls glowed in the darkness. They walked together until they came to the ridge were the path divided. From there, Brede had to walk through a gap and all the way down to the market place before reaching his farm. "Farewell, boy," he mumbled. "I will take my sons with me tomorrow and fetch that bear carcass." And then he added, "If you are a slave at the earl's farm, be sure and give my greetings to Una and her brother Vidur. They are distant relatives of my wife. Terrible that such proud folk must toil as slaves their whole lives."

"I am afraid," Reim whispered. "I am afraid to go back to the earl's farm."

Brede rubbed his beard. "Ya, a little slave boy is not worth much in situations like this. But you can't expect anything other than a beating, boy, when you fall asleep instead of tending to your sheep. I would give you a beating, too, if I had been your owner."

But then his voice grew milder, and he pinched Reim's cheek. "If it had been within my power, I would surely help you, boy, because I have always taken good care of my own two old slaves. But I am just a small farmer and have no influence with the earl or his warriors. For myself, I have been thinking of heading west, to Iceland. I am tired of all the warring in this land."

Reim gulped. He wanted to sing out, let me go with you, let me go with you to Iceland. But the words stuck in his throat. Deep inside, he knew that it was impossible. Instead, he thanked farmer Brede for his help and started down the wide horse path that wound west into the valley. He could hear his heart pounding in the night. "I won't go back!" he said loudly to himself. He stopped half-way and went into an abandoned stable. There he found some ropes to tie the sheep with. And then he dug himself down in the hay and fell asleep.

As soon as he awoke the next morning in the dilapidated stable, he knew that he was really in big trouble. They must have noticed that he was missing by now. For just a minute he thought of running away. He could untie the sheep and send them down into the valley. They would soon hear of the slaughtered sheep up on the mountain. The bear took the little slave boy too, they would think. They would not be able to find a trace of him anywhere.

But it did not take long before he started to waver. Would he be able to manage being alone for many days? It was not more than a day's hike to the market place and from there he could possibly get a ship. But then he would have to pass the barricades where the earl had set out watch posts. And what about Tir? He could not just leave her.

He poked about on the little forest path where he knew no one ever went. Just beneath him was the earl's farm. Out in the fields, the slave women walked back and forth cutting the grain. The fields glittered like gold in the brilliant sunshine. Down in the pasture he thought he could see Vidur, out looking after the horses.

Reim knelt down by the river that trickled past him, and drank in long slurps. When he lifted his head, he saw that the river banks were laden with juicy, red raspberries. They were so ripe that he only had to shake a bush to get a whole handful. Mmm-mmmmmmmm! Good! Reim felt the warm, sweet taste of summer all the way down to his toes.

He started. There was a rustling in the bushes just in back of him, and a half-grown boy ran out onto the path. Hosve, a lazy, dumb slave boy stood in front of him.

"Oh! It is you, Hosve," Reim said relieved. "You sure gave me a scare!"

Hosve's eyes narrowed treacherously. In his hand he had a knife.

"Hosve," Reim cried. "What is it?"

"Walk right in front of me down the path," Hosve said. "And don't try to turn back and look at me, or I will let you feel the blade of my sharp knife!"

They trod down the valley together in the baking evening sun.

"Here he is," Hosve said to the slave guard. "And don't forget to reward a faithful slave well!"

Vidur rose from his straw bed and went over to Reim. He lit a fish oil lamp. "Let me see your back!"

Reim lay on his stomach so he would not get any of the dry, sticking straw in the sores. His back burned as if glowing irons were pressed against his skin. He clenched his teeth. He did not want Vidur to see him cry.

Vidur's eyes turned black. "This must be the worst thing I have ever seen done to a child," he shouted in disgust. "Come and see how they treat the son of an Irish free farmer!"

Hosve hid in a dark corner of the room. Only Lut came pattering over to Reim, and stood looking at him with expressionless eyes. The others did not even bother getting up. Klegge stretched and yawned. "The son of an Irish free farmer," he croaked. "Since when can a slave start playing that he is a free man?" Old Klegge had been a slave for more than seventy winters. "My back is so thrashed that it only tickles when the whip bites. And I don't really care which dog does the biting. Old dogs have tough leather."

"Keep quiet, you old hound!" Vidur snapped. "I did not ask for your opinion!"

Klegge lay back in the hay. Soon afterwards, he snored as usual. Lut also returned to his place. They were all stiff and exhausted after a hard day's work out in the fields. Vidur rubbed some fat onto Reim's back. Even though he was as careful as he could be, Reim felt hot jets of fire shooting through his body.

"Lie still, boy," Vidur said briskly. His voice shook as he continued, "May the gods reward us poor slaves in our next life...."

———————————————

In the fall, the slave women returned from the mountain with the livestock. There was much commotion in the yard. Cows bellowed as the women ran back and forth placing all of the cheeses and butter in the storage house.

Una was restless. As soon as she had finished her work she slipped down the path that led to the sod house out in the forest.

Sigrid sat on a stony hill just above her little hut. Her three wild boys dashed between the trees playing vikings. They fought with their great wooden swords and could not help teasing their big sister. In the grass beside Sigrid laid a naked, little child kicking her feet in the air. She grasped her dainty, round toes and tried to put them in her mouth. The sun danced on her fair hair.

"Astrid!" Una exclaimed as she lifted her up and cuddled her tightly. "How she has grown, Sigrid! May Froya bless you for taking such good care of her while I have been away. Here!" she said as she threw several small leather pouches onto Sigrid's lap. "Some butter and cheese from the mountain dairy. I could not take more with me."

"Are you out of your mind, girl! Do you want to lose the other ear as well!"

Una quickly raised her hand to the left side of her head. She turned pale, but she did not say a word.

The three small vikings stormed towards them when they saw the leather pouches. They pleaded and begged.

"Hush," their mother scolded. "Not a soul must know where this food has come from. Or else we will all be in great trouble."

The boys nodded gravely. Sigrid smiled as she looked at them. The summer had given freckles and red cheeks. "We somehow got by this summer, too," she commented. They had managed to catch a bird every now and then and once they had even caught a hare. Tora went down to the cove every day to fish cod that they baked on the hearth. The forest was full of juicy berries and they gathered mushrooms and roots of all kinds. They already had a large store of dried nettle leaves and dandelions put away for the winter.

But how long could they get by in this way? Sigrid shrugged this heavy burden off her shoulders.

"And I have some strange news for you," she said. "Tora heard it. She has eyes and ears everywhere. One day an old man tottered up the slope to the earl's farm. He had just arrived on a ship from Iceland that had sailed across the sea to Norway to trade for timber and other necessary merchandise."

Now, it was not unusual for a foreigner to come to the earl's farm. All year long a steady stream of traders and merchants came to sell, wood carvers came to make wooden chests and wagons, and a smithy came to forge sharp weapons or beautiful ornaments. But this man was different. He walked right up to the slave quarters on the farm and asked for one of the earl's slaves, the one they called Digralde. When he heard that, the earl had taken this giant of a slave out on his viking mission, he seemed astonished. The stranger moved into a farm near the ship. He was going to wait for the return of the viking ships.

The slaves were out in the fields cutting grain when Tir shouted, "Look! Ships way out at the mouth of the bay!"

Reim spied out to sea. There was a strong wind out in the bay. The waves were topped with white caps. But Tir was right. Far, far out in the bay, the prows of dark tarred ships bobbed up and disappeared again, ploughing through of the frothy sea. The viking ships were on their way home from their expedition!

"They must have many treasures," Tir shouted. "And slaves...." Suddenly her face lit up. "Maybe there is someone who can tell us news of Ireland!"

Many of the others had seen the ships now. Down in the farmyard, folk hurried back and forth pointing excitedly towards the bay. The dogs barked nervously.

"No one will notice what the slaves do on a day like this," Reim said. And then they took a short cut through the forest to the inlet. A large group of people had already gathered. Hosve was there, and Lut, and old Kumba. Even Klegge had managed to drag himself down the hills, driven by a good portion of curiosity and two solid sticks. Una stood a bit away from the others. She was waiting for Digralde.

Sigurd sat on his little fallow-coloured horse, surrounded by the earl's warriors. He wore a belt with a silver buckle, and his hair was held back by a golden band tied around his forehead. He looked searchingly towards the ships approaching them. His mother stood talking to some of the other women from the larger farms. The women were dressed in snow white linen frocks with suspendered smocks, richly decorated with golden jewellery. The children were also dressed in their most beautiful, colourful clothing.

Shouts of jubilation rose as the first ship pulled into the inlet and the people on land could distinguish the forms of the men in the high poop. There was Arild and Torgrim and Svein. And there was Sigtrygg! As soon as they laid out the gang plank, children ran on board. Three small girls threw their arms around the neck of a shaggy, bearded viking. "Father, Father, let us see what you have brought home!"

They did not have wait very long. Soon the chests were carried onto land. Never had they seen such treasure! The chests were stuffed with gold, silver, precious jewels and expensive fabrics. The men dropped one of the chests as they tried to carry it onto land. Golden jewellery glittered in the sun, and the children hopped and jumped, laughed and danced excitedly.

A man came out of the ship carrying a large golden cross. The symbol of the Christian people! The people backed away in awe.

"Digralde!" Una was at his side.

"Good to see you again!" His eyes were filled with happiness. "Soon I will be a free man, Una. Free! Do you hear!" He lifted both her and the golden symbol up in the air, and the men around them laughed.

But where was the *Dragon*? Where was the earl's own ship? The women crowded around and demanded an answer.

The warriors shook their heads. They had been caught in a storm at high sea on their way home, and the ships had driven away from each other. But the *Dragon* would be coming soon. Such a strong ship would not be taken by a few breakers at sea.

The earl's wife grew pale when she heard this news. She mounted her horse and rode quickly away with her son.

"Here come the slaves," whispered Tir.

They all looked white and sick. And so many children! The smallest could not be more than five or six winters old. They were to be taken to the market place and sold there.

"Are any of you Irish?" Reim shouted at the flock.

"Yes, I am!" a little boy quickened in expectation when he heard his mother tongue.

"Do you know anything about our parents?" They named their parent's names and the name of the monastery there.

The boy shook his head. "I don't even know about my own parents and brothers and sisters," he said as he broke into sobs.

And then the whole flock was led down a path and into the hardwood forest, the leaves already shining a bright red and gold.

That evening all of the slaves gathered around Digralde in the slave quarters. And then he told them his story.

"This is the life!" he thought as he stood on the high poop of the ship, staring out over the sea glittering in the sun. The huge square sail flapped in the wind as the sea splashed over the deck. He felt intensely alive. This was the summer he had been waiting for. The viking summer!

There were nearly a hundred men on board the ship he was sailing with. Young boys, out on their first adventure, bustled about the deck, full of great expectation. They were all between twelve to fourteen years of age and most of them were the sons of great farm owners or chieftains. They were outfitted with many weapons and equipment. Some of them had expensive coats of mail and shining helmets. The leader of the flock was Narve, a muscular lad towering nearly a head above the others. He was exactly what a chieftain's son should be. His eyes were as sharp as a snake's and his golden hair hung down over his shoulders like a horse's mane. He was the strongest and most persevering at all sports. And he was greatly admired because of the golden down growing on his upper lip. But Digralde had noticed that when the waves grew too high, Narve hid in back of the ship's tent, bent over the railing, giving the contents of his stomach to the fish.

Digralde participated in almost everything that happened that summer. He saw villages and whole towns burned to the ground. He heard the terror-stricken cries of old people, women and children.

He saw people caged in and killed, and he saw young, strong women and men taken prisoner and dragged away.

But the vikings never talked about this when they gathered during the evenings. They amused themselves by counting the gold and silver coins that were stacked in their heavy chests. They tried on the heavy arm rings of golden metal. They boasted rowdily of their escapades. They told of Frankland and of Friesland and of all of the magnificent kingdoms westward. They spoke of impressive buildings, and of fine food and drink, and of all of the beautiful women at their command. When they were very drunk they would slap Digralde on the back and say that if he had not been a slave, they could very well have accepted him as leader. He was more than a head taller than the others and made a terrifying spectacle as he stormed ahead with his battle axe raised high in the air.

But thus far, Digralde had tried to keep in the background. It was as if his arms lacked the strength to raise his battle axe in slaughter.

He did not know why. Was he a coward? The whole time, a refrain filled with hope ran through his head: Get ahead, Digralde! This is your chance to accomplish a great deed! One single heroic deed and you are a free man, Digralde!

After their raids in the Irish sea, the viking ships sailed eastward. Soon they could see the cliffs of Frankland.

"The goddesses of fortune are with us." The earl went up on the poop deck. "We are nearing land!" he shouted. "I can see the village walls. Ready men! On with your weapons! Show them that you have viking blood in your veins!"

Digralde stood up and buckled his belt. He did not carry a sword, as the other free men, and he had no armour. His only weapon was a sharp battle axe and a long bow. His tunic was made of thick, reddish ox-hide, that could surely bounce off a few sharp arrows.

The vikings rowed to land and hid the ships under cover of some high bushes on the strand. Ship after ship glided into the dark inlet. Soon afterwards, the warriors swarmed out of the side of the ships, like a maze of armoured insects. Quietly, quietly, they crept up the banks towards the village walls.

The men used hooks and ropes to scale the walls of the village. From atop they could see out over the Frankish village, still slumbering in the dawning grey light. Farms were gathered in clusters along the narrow lanes, with stables and huts surrounding them. Out in the village pastures, black and white cows lay in the grass. Not a soul could be seen, other than a few drowsy hens scratching their claws on the fencing in the farmyards.

Digralde squinted. Far off, in back of a dense cluster of hardwood trees, the figure of a cross flashed at him in the morning light. It towered over the top of a sharply pointed roof, thrusting upwards into the heavens. Digralde knew that a cross signified treasures. He glanced around quickly to see if the other men had noticed it.

Then quite suddenly chaos broke out in the line just in front of him. One of the earl's warriors plunged forward and fell off the wall with an arrow in his chest. Soon afterwards another arrow pierced the shoulder of the warrior standing next to Digralde. So swift was the attack that the men completely lost control. Some of them leaped from the village wall and fled to the safety of their ships. A couple of twelve-year-olds started crying in shocked horror. The chieftain's son with the small, black snake-like eyes got an arrow right in his rear end and shrieked like a stuck pig. He hopped up and down in the bushes just below the village wall until he limped away to safety.

"By the help of Odin's eye, I can see from where the wind blows!" One of the vikings had crawled in back of a breast-work on the wall. He pointed towards an elevation in the middle of the village. There, the village men had barricaded themselves behind a the ruins of a house, weaponed with rocks and long bows. It was evident that the village had been visited by vikings or other pirates earlier that summer, because every man that could walk or crawl was armed to the teeth. Arrows swished through the air towards the vikings. Many of the earl's men swore and cursed. "This is the first time that this old viking has had to turn back and run with his tail between his legs," snarled BjOrn Viking. "And all because of some scabby Frankish townsmen. It is as if Odin himself has taught them to shoot with bow and arrow!" If they were not to end up in Valhalla earlier than they had intended, they would have to turn back and return to their ships.

Digralde must have been possessed. As the other men retreated, he wormed his way ahead, crawling flat on his stomach over the wall, and slipping down where the wall was lowest. Quick as lightning, he scuttled along the path that led through the bushes and towards the house with the cross figure. The whole time, he clutched his battle axe nervously.

When he reached the church wall, he lay down flat on his stomach again and crept into the shadow of an enormous tree. He broke out in a cold sweat. Around the church everything seemed quiet enough, but up in the hills a group of village men armed with poles and stone clubs appeared. Digralde had no time to waste. He had to move at once.

He ran across the church yard to the entrance and tore open the heavy oak door. The oppressive darkness inside blinded him. In the innermost part of the room, he caught sight of a pale light flickering in the draught of the open door.

A man, clothed in an ankle-length brown cloak, appeared before him. He had a silver cross on his chest. Beside him stood a boy in white, holding a lit candle in his hands. The boy's eyes were aghast in terror and anguish.

Digralde lost his temper in a flash. The man in brown was so tall and mighty that it would take too much time to go at him in a fair duel. Digralde lifted his axe and gave the man a deadly gash in the throat. He fell to the floor with a deadened thud.

But the boy stood frozen to the spot, blocking Digralde's way, his hands still tightly holding the candle against his white cloak. He had stiffened in fright.

A violent irritation weld up in Digralde. He heard the village men nearing and panicked with fear for his own life. He lifted his axe. One blow and the white creature fell lifeless onto the ground. The light extinguished with a slight puff.

He stepped over the two bodies in front of him on the floor and ran to the altar. Placed directly on the altar was a golden case and a silver goblet. Crowning the altar was a cross of heavy gold with brilliant, glittering stones. The christian god hung on the cross stiffly, his arms extended, his expression severe, staring directly at Digralde. Long shadows danced on the wall behind the cross. Digralde shuddered, feeling very uneasy. Maybe this really was a living god, this god that he had heard so much about. He must be powerful, since his people gathered such great treasures for him and gave him such wealth.

But Digralde did not have time to reason. He heard the tramping of many heavy feet just outside the church. Gathering all of his strength, he tore the cross off the wall. At that moment, the village men came through the west entry. Appalled, they moaned at the sight that stopped them—the two lifeless bodies on the ground.

Digralde escaped through a low door on the altar wall and crept through the thick bushes on the east side of the church wall. He soon had a whole flock of men at his heels. Rocks and arrows flew through the air. One of the rocks hit his shoulder, making him tumble. He pulled himself up again, clutching the crucifix tightly. He ran through a willow thicket and followed the low stone wall down to the strand. The viking ships were ready to sail, the oarsmen already at the oars.

Digralde ran aboard the *Dragon* and tumbled right into the earl's tent. The earl was in a ferocious temper. He had had to abandon the raid on the village. All that he had managed to plunder was a few small coins they had found in one of the houses. To the best of his memory, this was the worst day of his whole life.

"Out, slave!" he hissed at Digralde. He was ready to fling his drinking horn right into the face of this unbidden intruder.

Digralde pulled out the crucifix he had hidden under his cape. The room brightened, the golden ornamentation glittering brilliantly with precious jewels. The men backed away. The earl gasped, speechless. And then he threw himself back in his chair and laughed. He had never witnessed anything quite like this before, not in all of his years of raiding and plundering as a viking.

"All of you that are gathered here are men I have considered as the boldest in our land; and you all scattered like frightened hens at the first sight of some Frankish farmers! Look at him, this slave! He managed to plunder one of the holiest treasures of the church, right under the eyes of the Christians! There is more viking blood in the veins of this slave than there is in the whole lot of you! Come closer, Digralde. I thought you were a coward. But now I want everyone here to be witness: you are to be freed as soon as we return home and I can register it at the courts."

There was much commotion in the tent. The earl bade him drink, and all of the men paid tribute to the freed slave. The earl was finally in good humour again.

Free! Digralde thought as he tumbled into bed that night. Free! It was a strange feeling. He longed to return home at once. To Una. They had gone through so much together. He did not know how his child was faring, either. He could only hope for the best. Maybe he could start a new life; possibly earn a bit by hunting grouse or trapping falcons, so that he could buy Una out of slavery. They could build a small farm together, and there, their dear child could grow up.

But as his thoughts cleared, another child's face appeared out of the dark. A boy, only seven or eight winters old, standing with a lit candle in his hands. His sombre eyes grew and grew in the childish face.

Digralde twisted and turned in his bed, trying to escape these wide, staring eyes. He was bathed in sweat. It was as if this boy lived inside of him, would not let him go. "Thor," he moaned. "Save me from this torment. This is worse than any nightmare!"

"Quiet, dumb dog!" one of his fellow mates snarled. "Being a free man does not give you the right to disturb a good night's sleep for us others!" He pulled his sheepskin rug over his head, and fell asleep again, as the sea rolled on and the ship sailed forward to new places.

I have paid a high price for my freedom, Digralde thought. And then he did something that he had not done since he was six winters old and was sold into slavery. He rolled over on his side and cried.

The day after the viking fleet had returned home, the slave women walked down the steep path that led to the washing place. Tir carried a basket of clothes that was larger than herself. She held herself upright by leaning on a cane. Behind her came Kumba and Una carrying a pot of boiling water. They set the basket and pot of water down by the mouth of the river. "Ish! What a stink!" Kumba said as she pinched her nose. She backed out into the water as she loosened the rope binding the sack of clothing. The clothes were stiff with dried-in dirt. She dumped the whole lot out onto the flat rocks: tunics, leggings and capes. All were the same grey-brown colour.

One of the girls placed her hands on her hips and snickered, "And they call themselves the great vikings! They can boast of their heroic deeds, but there is nothing as dismal in this whole world as their filthy underclothes!"

Kumba hooted. "Just now, the same men are sitting in the hall, drinking their mead, and beating their chests. But things would not go well for this viking army if they did not have us lowly slave women to clean up the dirt after them. We are the only ones that do not sit gaping at their stories!"

The slave women laughed, their laughter mingling with the murmur of the waterfall behind them.

Una beat the clothes with a board, sending echoes bounding along the mountain walls surrounding them. "That is the way to do it, girl!"

Tir washed a jacket that, to start with, just resembled a dried-up ball of soil and dirt. She thought she saw blotches of dried blood. She had to tear at the material and beat it before she could even distinguish the colour. It was a beautiful jacket with woven golden threads. Had it been stolen off a dead man? Tir shuddered.

The water sparkled green and icy cold in the low autumn sun. Here and there, small schools of fish darted between the rocks, out towards the sand banks. Tir waded out and started with the linen clothing. It was nearly impossible to get them clean. She beat them and beat them, until her fingers and feet were frozen stiff. Una had to come out and help her.

And then finally, row upon row of the vikings' red, green and blue tunics and white linen trousers blew in the wind.

"Håvard Viking has really got wind in his sails now," the girls giggled, when they saw Håvard's trousers fill with wind and nearly blow off the line and out to sea.

The trip up the steep river bank was easier without the heavy load. From the earl's hall they heard laughter and commotion. All the earl's relatives were gathered there, awaiting the arrival of the *Dragon*. Posted in many positions around the yard, the warriors stood watch. They knew that rumours of the fantastic treasures the fleet of ships had returned with would spread quickly.

An old, bent man stumbled up the path to the slave quarters. "Isn't that the foreigner that came on the merchant's ship from Iceland?" one of the girls asked.

"Yes," Tir nodded. "Wonder what he wants...."

Three whole days, the earl's son sat rigidly on his horse, looking out towards the sea until the sun sank behind the fir tree ridges in the west.

"Sigurd!"

The earl's son turned. His face lit up. "Is it you, Reim!" He jumped down and led his horse over to a tree. And then he stuck his hand inside his cloak and pulled out a little object he had hidden there.

Reim's eyes filled with wonder. Sigurd was holding a miniature ship with a golden dragon's head and golden shields placed along the side of the ship.

"It is the *Dragon*," Sigurd said proudly. "I learned how to carve the ship from the wood carver that was here at the farm this past winter. Mother gave me a piece of silk for the sails. And then I got the smithy to nail the shields...."

"It is a wonderful ship!" Reim said.

The sea had washed a puddle of water up onto the slope of naked rock. The boys lay down on their stomachs and blew wind into the sails of the little ship, making waves on the surface of the puddle with sticks they splashed in the water. The little dragon ship sailed the length of the puddle at least a hundred times, in and out of every inlet, the sail reflecting on the surface of the water.

"Now we set off on a viking raid!" Sigurd blew at the ship so his cheeks puffed out like a bellow. "Out to plunder gold and treasures of silver," he shrieked, swinging his little axe over his head. "To foreign coastlines! Out to capture young slaves!"

But as soon as the words had escaped his lips, he bit them. "Let's find something else to do," he said quickly.

"What?"

Sigurd lowered his voice secretively. "We could blend our blood and become blood brothers forever."

"Blend blood?" Reim shuddered.

"Yes, look here. I cut myself on the finger, and them you do the same. If we blend our blood we become blood brothers in life and death!"

Sigurd took out his knife and gave it to Reim. "You first!"

The sharp iron against his soft skin make Reim sick. But he could not get out of this. He shut his eyes and cut. A thin stripe of blood trickled down his thumb. "Hurry now!" he shouted excitedly. "Before all my blood runs out!"

Sigurd gritted his teeth and tried to imitate the tough, hard faces of his father's warriors. He pricked his finger with the sharp knife and pressed out a drop of blood.

Reim and Sigurd stared gravely into each other's eyes as they pressed their two thumbs together.

"Never fail," said Sigurd solemnly.

"Never fail."

This was so serious, goose bumps rippled down their backs.

Then the sun sank down behind the fir tree ridge, and the air turned frigid. Sigurd stuck his knife back into his belt and got up. He fetched his little horse, and Reim jumped up in back of him. They rode at full trot through the woods until they came to the place where the path divided. Reim jumped off.

Sigurd looked at him thoughtfully as each started on his own way. "I am not really sure that it was right of me to blend my blood with a slave," he said. "I just hope that the gods were not looking."

Reim laughed. "Your gods are surely asleep after having fought the whole day long in the fields near Valhalla."

Reim ran lightly up the hill to the slave quarters. As he entered, he saw a foreign man sitting by the hearth.

"What do you want with me?" Digralde growled.

There was nothing stately or proud about the sunken figure on the bench. He sat bundled up in a russet brown cape worn by the poor farmers. His hands were calloused and rough after many years of hard work on the land. Digralde looked down at the bowed head and thin, white hair that curled around his ears. He waited impatiently. "State your business, old man," he repeated.

When the man finally lifted his head, Digralde looked directly into a pair of eyes that had the same colour as the sea on a hazy summer day. He started. Deep in those eyes he saw a little boy, led by the enormous, comforting hand of his father. They struggled up the steep hills to the big farm, went into the great hall and stood in front of the high seat; the earl's high seat. There the father let go of the little hand, and the boy saw the gleam of a piece of silver. "What is it, Father?" The father turned his back to the boy and left. "Father, Father, answer me!" But a back holds no answers. It just grew smaller and smaller. It was as if the figure just floated away and disappeared, never to return, like in some weird, evil nightmare.

Since then, Digralde had hated his father, carrying his seething bitterness deep inside. His father, with such mighty shoulders, such strong arms, a father he had trusted, had left him without as much as a word.

Digralde was confused. Now this bit of a man sat in front of him. He both was, and was not, the father he knew and remembered.

The old man got up and walked slowly, hesitantly, over to his son. "More than fifteen years have passed since we last saw each other, son. If it had not been for your fair, curly hair I might never have recognized you."

"Yes, I have grown up to be both mighty and bold," Digralde snarled. "But my strength comes from day after day of carrying and dragging heavy grey boulders. I dug in the earth with my bare hands and dragged wagon loads that even a work horse would balk at. These past fifteen years I have worked harder than any beast."

His father crumpled wearily. "Try to understand, my son. Listen to what an old man has to tell you. No one is more unhappy about what happened than I am. Once, I was a fairly well-situated farmer with a young and kind wife. Our farm was on a sun-filled slope, and it had been handed down from father to son for three generations. We did not have great fields, but what we had was easy to work and fruitful. I got up every morning before the rooster call, ploughed the earth, sowed, and gathered feed for our cows, cut the grain, and brought it in to the stable. My hands were as heavy as rocks by evening, but I was in good humour. We had five healthy children, and we managed to take good care of them all. You were the oldest son, and bigger and stronger than the others."

"And then a catastrophe befell us. It had been a bad year throughout the whole district. We barely managed to gather enough food to tide us through the winter."

"Thieves hid in the forest and at night they crept up to our farm. I heard the horses' hooves in our yard and got up to see. Grain thieves! It would have been mad to try and defend ourselves against such men. In the light of the moon I could see them drag sack after sack of grain from the storage house and lift them up onto the horses' backs. But I had to thank the goddesses of fortune that we escaped with our lives. My wife and children all slept safely. But down in the village many of the farms were burning. The whole valley was in flames."

"And then came hunger. It was a disastrous year for our area. No one had enough food. We peeled the bark off the trees and cooked our meals out of roots and leaves. I borrowed a few barrels of grain, and went into debt to one of the great land owners. First, I had to give up the fields and the land that my father himself had cleared. Later, I did not even own the house that we lived in. I tossed and turned during the night, listening to my children whimpering and crying for food. The two youngest died that winter. Only Odin himself knows how I have suffered!"

"And then I took you by the hand and led you away. My heart bled that day. But I had no choice. You were big and strong, and you could save your other brothers and sisters."

"I received a piece of silver. The silver I exchanged for grain. I sold you as a farmer sells a calf at market. But you saved our lives for the time being. I thought that when this horrible year was over, I would be able to buy you free."

"And then I begged a place for us on a ship to Iceland. I had relatives there that would hopefully help us. But the goddesses of fortune had turned their backs on us. My kind wife and all of my children died of exhaustion before we reached Iceland. I was so sick, I was not of much use to my Icelandic kinsmen during my first months in this new land. But they helped me as much as they could. I built a small farm there. That has taken me most of my lifetime. And the whole time that I was working in Iceland I thought of you: I had to free my son from slavery."

The old man rested his head in his hands. "Try to understand, my son!"

Digralde answered bluntly, "You are too late. Your slave son has won his own freedom."

His father looked at him in amazement. Digralde continued, "When the earl returns, he is going to go to the courts and acknowledge that I am a free man."

Digralde sat down on the bench beside his father. "The only tie I have to this slave house is the slave girl whom I want for my wife. I must get her out of slavery also." He drew Una down beside him on the bench and pulled back her hair. "You can see for yourself what a slave woman had to endure to scrounge food for her own child."

The old man moved away, shaking his head. Digralde leaned towards him. His voice was milder. "We two will manage. But our little daughter, Astrid, is being fostered by a poor widow. If you want to do me a favour, use that silver of yours to buy a room for Sigrid and her children on your ship. Be sure that little Astrid is well taken care of in Iceland."

Seven days and seven nights later, a ship with a broken prow steered into the bay. It was the *Dragon*.

The ship had blown onto the shore of Sweden during a storm. There, they had fought against the Swedish vikings, and nearly all of the vikings from the *Dragon* had fallen to Swedish swords.

"My husband is dead!" the earl's wife cried, stretching her arms towards the heavens. "Cursed be the goddesses of fortune and destiny on a day such as this!"

"The earl is dead," Kumba crooned, her eyes sparkling like clumps of golden amber. "I finally got him! My curses and spells have triumphed!"

But Digralde's eyes turned dark as he bowed his head. Now he would always be a slave. And he would have to continue slaving. The earl was dead and could not proclaim at the courts that he was to be a free man.

The days that followed were a turmoil. Never before had there been such commotion and bustle just because someone had died. The whole farm smelled of the advent season, even though they were barely into the fall. The women baked and cooked, and the men brewed. The slaves toiled from morning to late at night, and hardly had time to close their eyes before it was time to start anew. Those that made the food had one great advantage; they could run off with something to eat every now and then. Una fell asleep well fed and satisfied every evening now. "Never do we have such good days as when someone dies," she sighed contentedly.

Old Klegge dwelled in the cellar where they were brewing the mead. He grew more and more lively with every passing day, as he danced around on unsteady legs, singing merry songs. Finally the earl's wife protested and sent him out to the large cooking house to help knead the dough. He enjoyed being there also. There were so many women and girls to show off for, and he was quick to pinch their cheeks.

A gravesite had been chosen high up on a ridge overlooking the bay. The earl's wife had paid for twelve slaves from a neighbouring farm to help with the burial. All in all, twenty-two men dug and dug for three days on end. "Quite a grave for just one man," Tir commented. "Can you understand, Reim?"

But they soon understood. The day after the grave digging was finished, they heard heavy rhythmic sighs and shouts from men dragging something of enormous weight. The servants, slave girls and craftsmen at the farm ran out of the houses, the children at their heels. Down on the strand the slaves were dragging the *Dragon* onto land. The ship resembled a monstrous, sick sea bird as it lay on the beach, seeming to gasp for air. Slowly, nearly imperceptibly, the ship inched forward, as the men dragged the keel over rolling logs. The slaves' murmuring, a dark, monotone elegy, resounded across the bay and over the fields. By evening, many were hoarse. But then the ship had been placed in the grave.

The women and children started carrying things on board the ship. They carried chests and trunks, barrels of food, pots and pans and spits. They dragged heavy wagons and sleds. From sun up until sun down, a steady stream of people ran between the houses and the grave. In the farmyard, two oxen and some sheep squalled and bellowed as they were led to slaughter. And late that evening, the eerie neighing of a young stallion felled by an axe sounded through the farmyard.

Just as the moon rose over the horizon, a procession carrying the earl advanced towards the ship. The earl was clothed in a red cape and his sword and shield were placed on top of him, as was the custom for the burial of a mighty warrior. Now he was to start out on the long journey to Odin at Valhalla. Hired mourners wailed, stretching their hands towards the heavenly lights slowly rising over the tops of the fir trees, colouring the landscape a ghastly silver.

Shovel after shovel of earth was thrown onto the mighty grave mound. Reim sneaked away. Exhaustion felt like a heavy weight in his body. If he could slip away now, he might be able to steal at least a few minutes sleep. No one would notice that he was gone. He ran down the path that led to the field with the ancient oak tree.

He was startled to hear a strangled hiccoughing just beside him. He jumped aside. A boy sat right under the oak tree, his fair head leaning against his knees, his shoulders shaking. Sigurd! The earl's son who was such an expert in the use of weaponry and warring! The earl's son who was to go on the viking mission next summer! He sat crying and sobbing! Reim walked over to him and put his arm around Sigurd's shoulders. Sigurd started and looked up at Reim with a tear striped face. He quickly hid his eyes in his hands again.

"I can understand how sad you must be because your father is dead."

Sigurd lifted his head. His voice was low, almost a whisper. "I am thinking about Fakse. Why did they have to take my horse from me? We played together every single day. Now Fakse is dead and buried...." His sobbing turned to a harsh cry.

Reim sat down close beside Sigurd. A good feeling took hold of him. Here they were, a slave and an earl's son. Both of them were eleven winters old, and they both had the same feelings deep down in their hearts. Reim could visualize the little stall at home in Ireland. Stella, he thought. My good, fine horse. I will never see you again either.

Sigurd wiped his nose on the back of his hand. "When I come home from the viking raids and am considered grown up, Reim, I am going to free both you and your sister."

And then he laughed mockingly. "You know, Reim, I am the earl on this farm now. As a matter of fact, I own six large farms and have command of more than thirty slaves. Everyone expects me to be a great viking. But all I really want to do is carve wooden figures like the wood carver does." He smiled wryly. "Father made a mistake in naming me after Sigurd, the Dragon Slayer." Sigurd spread his cloak out on the ground, and the boys lay back against the thick trunk of the oak tree. Reim did not know if he dared believe what Sigurd had said. Free?!! He dreamed that he was home playing in the fields of Ireland. Far, far, away he heard the sorrowful, drawn out chanting. It grew fainter and fainter until, at last, it completely died away.

Digralde stumbled about, mumbling and grumbling. When he was in that humour no one dared talk to him. They went out of their way to avoid him, careful not to induce one of his temper tantrums.

But then he livened up. He called for Vidur and Una. "The earl is dead," he whispered. "This could be our only chance. Rumours of the treasures we brought home from our raids in the west have spread to our neighbouring districts. Riches always make for unrest. If I am not wrong, we can expect an attack at any time now. And while the great folk are busy fighting, they will not be watching what the slaves are up to...."

The only one that heard them talking that evening was Reim. He lay still, his heart drumming, trying to hear every word that was said. The day after, he stole over to Digralde and said, "Can I be with you on the journey you talked about?"

Digralde glared at him, aghast. Then he shook him by the shoulders until Reim thought his head would rattle off. "Does anyone else know about this, boy? Answer me!"

"N-n-no," Reim stammered, struggling to free himself.

"What you heard was not meant for your ears," Digralde said gruffly. "We cannot drag a whole flock of children with us on such a dangerous mission."

But he must have noticed that the last ray of hope disappeared from Reim's eyes, because a minute later he tousled his hair, and said, "All right, boy. I cannot really forbid you to follow, can I? But you keep quiet about this, do you hear!" he threatened, his eyes growing dark.

All of those who knew of the plan had to be on guard constantly. As soon as any unusual movement was noticed in the forest near the farm, the others had to be told at once. They accumulated as much food as possible; a little bread, a little flour and a bit of dried meat. Tir crept over to the slave quarters at night to sleep.

They waited in hope. Night after night, the full moon shone over the sleepy cluster of houses and warriors standing guard at their posts. The ocean glittered like a giant shield of silver. Now and then, faint sounds from the dark forest broke the silence of the night. Was it a spy? No, just a squirrel hopping lightly from branch to branch or a bird flying over the crown of a tree. Not as much as the shadow of a human being to see.

After some days, the guards started to relax. There were fewer men on each watch. And the men changed guard directly with others from the festivities in the great hall. They had much to celebrate now, with food and drink. The young boy who had just become earl sat in the high seat beside his mother, acknowledging every man that would fall on his knees before him. Everyone agreed that this tall, fair-haired boy would be a worthy chieftain. And he would surely win the allegiance of many men as time wore on. Bold warriors were always attracted by piles of gold.

Digralde's plan, in essence, was to get on board one of the ships bound for Iceland late that fall. Farmer Brede and Una were distantly related, and Brede was planning to leave for Iceland. If they claimed to be Brede's slaves they just might get onto the ship also. It was a daring plan, but Digralde clung to it as a lice clings to a straw.

If only it was not too late. The air seemed to have an icy bite to it already. Another winter slaving under the earl's warriors would not be bearable.

Digralde stood between Tir and Reim, watching the last of the leaves whirl to the ground. Bare branches grasped towards the heavens, naked, desolate. Suddenly Digralde bent down.

"What are you looking for, Digralde?"

Digralde took Tir's arm and pointed. There was a thin, icy membrane covering the clay earth after a frosty night. But at one spot, just under the clear surface, they could see a movement, so delicate, like the fragile remnants of summer. Digralde crushed the thin ice, and a butterfly whirled out of its hiding place. At first, the wings flapped slowly, but it soon flew away into the clear autumn air.

"It will die anyway," Tir said. "Maybe this evening."

"Yes," Digralde said thoughtfully, as he watched the transparent wings flutter and disappear into the air. "But it will die free."

Digralde bowed his head and went back to the slave's quarters. Tir and Reim knew that this would be the last night he would stand watch.

PART III

"*D*igralde!" Reim whispered. "Listen!"

The giant grunted in his sleep and waved his arms, sending straw flying throughout the air. "Who dares wake a worn-out slave? I should be sleeping," he snorted. "Quiet in this room, or I'll tear the roof down over your heads."

"Digralde," Reim repeated tugging at his great beard. "I heard noises outside!"

Digralde shot out of bed. He tore the rag out of the little peek hole in the wall and spied out into the dismal, dark-blue night. The fir forest cast shadows, black and dreary, across the farmyard. But if his senses were not tricking him, he thought he heard the clashing of weapons.

At that moment, the clouds flew across the sky, exposing a bright, beaming moon. And then he saw them. A long row of men, sneaking like grey wolves towards the earl's house. They were heavily armed with swords and shields and sharp battle axes. Long spears gleamed, half concealed in the thicket. The horsemen waited there.

"By the god of thunder, you are right," Digralde exhaled. "Wake the others. We have to get going."

Five slaves had planned to escape. They fetched their cloth bundles and dressed without as much as a word. Soon they were ready.

Reim bent over Kumba. He saw that her face was wet. "Old Kumba will miss you all," she said. "But go on your way now!"

Klegge grunted from his corner of the room. "You are all mad, running from one master to the other. But may the gods fare well with you."

The slaves ducked under the low door frame, out into the black night. There were no guards to be seen.

A horn sounded.

The Illuges attacked! The slaves threw themselves flat into the shadow of some hazel bushes. For one short moment they witnessed the vicious fighting out in the farmyard. The first arrows hit the guards in the yard. Soon afterwards, the earl's men swarmed out of their sleeping rooms. They woke with a start as they saw the intruders, and quickly climbed up to the roof of the hall, sending a rainstorm of arrows towards the attackers.

Soon afterwards, the sound of thundering hoofs invaded the yard. The Illuge horsemen rode out of the protective darkness and surrounded the whole yard. Arrows and spears pierced the air, shot from tree tops and thick bushes.

The earl's men had barricaded themselves upon the roof of the hall, and now had their hands full with stopping the flying, flaming torches that flew like blazing stars in the darkness. The fire caught on the dry sod roofs over the sleeping quarters, and soon afterwards, the storage house went up in flames. The red fire slicked over the ridge on the roof. Reflections from the fire flickered across the log walls of the great hall.

"Now! Run!" Digralde whispered. "We have to get to the ferry. Since the Illuges have arrived here, they must have cleared the way for us. Come!" He scurried like an animal across the dewy grass. The others followed.

Reim watched as the dark, crawling figures hurried away from the slave quarters. He knew that he should follow closely behind them and get away from the farm quickly. But something held him back. I am quick on my feet, he thought. I will catch up with them. And he knew the way like the back of his hand. He had accompanied Digralde down to the ferry landing before. The ferryman was a freed slave from the earl's farm.

Reim lay as quiet as a mouse in his hiding place and watched the violent fighting. Men and horses fell over each other out in the yard. Wild cries and enraged cursing mingled with the miserable wailing of the wounded. The flames crackled and snapped as they devoured the houses. For a while, there was great danger that the flames would spread to the forest, but the wind shifted.

The earl's men fought well, and soon the battle ended. The Illuges realized that they would not be able to win the seat of the earldom in one quick battle. They dragged their prisoners and wounded back into the cover of the thicket. A deathly quiet fell over the yard. In the pale moonlight lay the lifeless bodies of horses and men.

"But Sigurd is safe," Reim commented aloud to himself. "Blood brothers in life and death! Now I had better hurry after the others."

He ran quickly through the forest and came to the barricade the earl's men had set up at one of their watch posts. His heart pounded in his chest. The time he had gone through the forest with Digralde, and they had been stopped here. One of the watchmen had followed them the rest of the way to make sure that they did not go any further than the ferry landing. But this time he had little to fear from the earl's warriors. Behind the stony barricade he caught sight of the bodies of the dead watchmen. They lay in a pile, one upon the other, with arrows still in their backs.

Reim ran like a frightened deer, hopping over roots and rocks. The path in front of him was dark and silent. Not a sign of the others. He cursed himself for having waited. The black of night closed in on him. He was completely alone.

The wind whistled and sighed through the tops of the great fir trees. "Are you afraid?" the fir branches seemed to whisper as they swished and swayed.

"Yes, I am so scared," answered his throbbing heart. "The forest is full of spirits and trolls. They can lead me astray, maybe lure me into their mountain kingdom...."

"Hussssssssh! One does not speak of that," the wind howled.

The sky behind the tall tree tops brightened in pale greenish tones, but the forest floor was pitch black. He could hear a soft gurgling in the distance.

That must be the river. A path followed the river all the way down to the inlet, west of the forest ridge. As long as the clouds darkened the moon, he would have to feel his way through the forest. He caught a glimpse of the tall cliff on the west side of the path, and knew that he was on the right way.

Suddenly a sharp howl cut the air. Reim felt his blood freeze in his veins. Was it the dogs from the farm out searching for escaped slaves, or perhaps wolves? The moon broke through the thick covering of clouds and for a moment, the path shone white before him in the sharp light. He ran faster. Branches thrashed his face. He was down in the valley now, among the heather and tall, yellow ferns. Just as the moon disappeared again, he heard another howl. Closer this time. He stood stock still, until the moon again broke through. And then he ran for all he was worth, following the white path, weaving around the tree trunks, hopping over rocks and branches, slipping at times on the wet moss. He pulled himself up and continued running until sweat poured like rain drops down his face.

A howl sounded just beside him. And then a whole chorus of howling split the night.

There they are, a frightened, panicking voice inside of him said. There!

In the sharp moonlight, he could see three or four wolf-like figures, staring at him with evil, yellow eyes. But the slinking shadows to the rear of them scared him more. They were not the shadows of animals! They were people! Now he knew he had been followed. He could not be sure if he had been followed by the earl's warriors or the Illuges' men. But he knew that it was considered greatly profitable to capture runaway slaves.

Blood pounded against his forehead. A sob weld up in his chest. He might just as well throw himself down on the path and give himself up. Give up this whole mad flight of his. But he could not go back. He shuddered to think of the whipping that had awaited him when he had lost the sheep in the mountains.

The moon disappeared again and Reim set off, running at random through the bushes and mossy swamplands. He thought he felt the snapping of the dogs at his neck. Finally, he reached the river. He jumped. The icy water splashed on his face giving him renewed strength. He swam over to the other side, and hid behind a fir tree that had fallen into the water. There he lay deathly still. He hardly dared to breathe. The wolf-like dogs reached the river banks, howled and sniffed at the place where his tracks disappeared. Then the men came into sight. They waded out into the river, swearing at this prey that had outsmarted them. They searched for hours, but in the end they gave up. Were they waiting for him in the bushes on the edge of the river bank? Reim did not know for sure. He felt how bitingly cold the river water was, but he stayed hidden under the tree roots until daylight shimmered in the early morning and a frosty mist settled over the river. Then he knew if he did not crawl up to the river banks he would soon freeze to death. His body was already stiff and blue.

He dragged himself along the great tree trunk and pulled himself up onto the river bank. There he lay, completely exhausted, on the rocky strand, until he saw the sun rise over the mountain ridge. He pulled himself up on his elbow and threw off his wet clothing. Now that the morning mist had evaporated, he could see a wide, green field right next to the strand. A whole flock of sheep grazed there. He must have run all the way across the valley, and was now on the side where the Illuges lived. "But I am still free!" he announced aloud to himself. The rays of the pale autumn sun warmed him like a good friend. He crawled across the field and huddled down beside one of the warm animals lying on the ground. There he fell into a deep sleep and did not even notice when a pair of strong arms picked him up and carried him away.

When Reim awoke, he looked directly into two pairs of curious eyes. On one side of him stood a stocky, short man with a shabby beard, and on the other side, a hunched-over, little woman with corn-gold braids hanging down on her bosom.

"Don't you be afraid now," said the woman. Her smiling eyes were a heavenly blue. "We are not going to hurt you. Look here," she said as she held out a bowl with something warm and sweet. "Drink some of this goat's milk. It will help you get your strength back."

Reim took the bowl and drank in greedy gulps.

"The poor boy," the man said. "You were half frozen to death when I found you early this morning down by the river banks. You have slept the whole day. Something great has happened north in the valley this past night. We saw the flames licking over the edge of the forest, and even now there is a lot of smoke in the air. Was it Earl Hakon's farm that burned? Yes, because we know, of course, that you are an escaped slave."

Reim sat up with a start.

"You have nothing to fear here," the wife repeated, trying to calm him. "You have come to the right place, for even if we are slaves to the Illuge farm, it is still our duty as human beings to help those that are in need. We are lucky enough to have our own little farm. But still, we cannot hide you here much longer."

Reim looked around. He wouldn't call this little hut a farm. It wasn't anything more than a little shed built of earth and stone, with a fallen-in moss grown roof. The only bed in the room was the one he was sitting on. A little goat wandered around the hut, eating bits of moss off the walls.

Reim turned his head quickly. He was sure that he had heard a weak voice from the corner of the room. There was a pile of old rags and a sheepskin, but now he saw the pile stir a bit, and a shrivelled head stuck out of the rags. It was a very old man. His face was as yellow and withered as a turnip that has lain the whole winter through. Reim sprang from his bed. One really couldn't be sure that goblins and such didn't live in a place like this.

"Did I scare you?" the old man piped. He chuckled and laughed like a little trickling stream. "Here you see a creature about as ancient as Odin himself. Old people have so many memories. Just come a bit closer, you...."

Reim ventured a bit nearer. The old man struggled to sit up. The woman packed a roll of sheepskins behind his back and pulled him up enough so his head reached over the top of the pile of rags. "So, so now, Great-grandfather," she said.

"We will soon have something to warm your old carcass, dear old creature."

The old man smiled a toothless grin. "Very seldom do we see young people in this room. When I see a young fellow like yourself, I remember my own first years as a slave. They say that my parents were free farmers, but I can't even remember their faces. I was four or five winters old when I was stolen from their farm and made a slave. A kind, old slave woman fostered me.

As long as I have lived in this land, I have been a slave. My wife was a slave here on the Illuge Einarsson farm. And all thirteen of our children were slaves and all of my grandchildren and great-grand-children too. They were born slaves, and they died as slaves. That is the will of God."

Reim felt tears welling up in his eyes and turned away. And as such it will be with Tir and myself if we don't get away from this country, he thought.

"But I have had a good life as a slave," the old man continued. "As long as no one decides to beat us to death, we live longer, slaving, than the great men live, with their warfaring. During my years, I have slaved under twelve different masters. All of them got their heads cut off somewhere in a foreign land. I had to work hard, that's true, but my head has always sat safely and securely on my shoulders, thank goodness. The only thing it is useful for now is predicting the weather, based on my gout, ha, ha, ha. But then I have seen the flowering of the white anemone in the forest nearly a hundred times."

Reim swallowed. "If I have slept as long as you say, then I am afraid that I have to get going as soon as possible."

The woman came with the clothes she had dried by the fire. She pointed through the open door. "You can see the ferry landing from here. May the goddesses of fortune be with you, my dear boy." And then she added quietly, so that Reim barely heard it, "But a little slave like you, running around here alone, doesn't stand much of a chance!"

The sun was slowly sinking behind the horizon as Reim ran down the bank to the ferry landing. He ran barefooted, his woollen jacket trailing behind him. Anyone could see that he was a slave but still, he hoped with all of his might that this would work out. Down in the bay, there was the small rowboat that freighted people over the sound, a narrow neck of water. That meant that the ferryman was at home. He let his breath out in relief.

The little log house lay right at the water's edge. He could see the tall, stooped figure of the ferryman in the door opening. Reim felt relief bubbling up in his chest. He was nearly safe. Just across the sound was the market place, and from there he could make his way to Brede's farm. He ran as lightly as a hare the last part of the way to the ferryman's house.

"I have to get over to the market place!" he cried, out of breath. "Please take me over. If you will, you can have this cross as payment." He showed him the little iron cross he had hanging from a chain around his neck.

Just then Reim realized that something was wrong. The ferryman tried to warn him, give him a sign, make him understand that he should run away.

"You shouldn't have come here," he whispered as he waved his arms.

But it was too late. Two men appeared in the door opening. Reim jumped. He recognized his two pursuers from the night before. The dog, just inside the door, snapped and barked.

"Could just be that we can give you a free ride over to the market place." One man laughed ominously, sticking his knife against Reim's ribs. "We have made some big catches during the night, but small fish pay off, too."

Reim looked around. Inside the shanty, he caught sight of three of the earl's warriors. They stood in their underwear, with their hands bound behind their backs. They did not look especially dignified any more. One prisoner had a yellow goat's beard and rat-like eyes. Reim shrank away from his stare. Orm Viking!

"Out with you three, or we'll set a fire under your feet," the men from the Illuge family commanded.

And then they set the dogs on the ferryman and asked him to consider, once again, if he would row them over to the market place.

Reim had pictured the market place as being much larger. He was quite disappointed. There were no large stone buildings, just a group of low wooden stalls with scorched turf roofs. Between the stalls were miserable, muddy alleys, where sticky, golden autumn leaves pasted themselves to the earth.

But Kumba had been right about the activity at the market place. The muddy alleys were bulging with people, and from the shops, loud shouts and cries could be heard. Some of the tradesmen sold pots and pans; others sold snow-white feathers to fill the bedclothing of the rich. A falconer stood showing off his gleaming, black birds, holding them with a leather glove. The clothing tradesmen drew forth bundle after bundle of clothes and colourful materials from their overflowing chests. Thick, grey smoke rose through the roof of the blacksmith's. The forge smouldered and glowed, and the strokes of his hammer were deafening. There were many animals about, too. Cackling hens and grunting pigs scurried through the alleys. People from the larger farms rode between the stalls on horses decorated with golden harnesses. The children rode on small, ragged horses and laughed, delighted with all of the strange sights at the market.

At the edge of the market area, women set up tents of skin. Here they brewed herbal drinks for the frozen travellers. "We are clairvoyant," they called hoarsely. "We can tell your fortune! We can foretell the future and all that has happened since the beginning of this world!"

With them was a little, round-bellied man with quick eyes. He sold various tokens of luck that could be hung around the neck or be used as an arm ring. He took out several small silver hammers and jingled them before the eyes of the people passing by. "Look! Here are Thor's powerful hammers," he tempted. "They will protect you against spirits and goblins!"

A man, broken by gout, stopped to buy one.

The tradesman winked slyly, and from the folds in his coat fetched forth a little gleaming cross. He spied around quickly. "You should buy this too, old friend," he whispered confidentially. "That bent back of yours won't get better until you use more powerful magic. This cross token is just the thing now in the West. They say that it will bring health and long life."

The old man dug deep into his leather pouch and paid with another piece of silver.

Slaves were also sold at the market place.

Beside Karl Jarlshovde, from the Illuge family, stood Reim, his heart pounding painfully in his chest. Scattered throughout the area were many women, children and grown men. Most of them were tied with ropes. The buyers paced back and forth through the crowd, inspecting the slaves and making their deals with the sellers.

Strong young boys were in demand, but many wanted slave girls, too. They were cheaper.

"Open your mouth," commanded a huge man who stopped in front of Reim. He had a frothy, grey-black beard and his eyes were nearly hidden under bushy eyebrows. Reim did not dare not disobey him. He opened his mouth wide, and stared up towards the bleached autumn sun, hanging in the air over the slave market.

The man chuckled. "This lad knows enough to bite back, even though he is right in the process of losing his baby teeth!"

"I am sure you were not looking for a watchdog anyway, were you?" laughed Karl Jarlshovde.

The man inspected Reim from top to toe. "He won't be able to do much hard work. He is too skinny and weak," he finally said. "Not much power in those bird's wings." He squeezed Reim's forearm.

"But he can grow up to be big and strong, dear friend. You shouldn't judge a six winters' colt by its walk."

The farmer threw his head back and laughed. "You are just one big salesman, you are, Karl Jarlshovde. You probably want me to think that this man isn't weaned yet. Anyone can see that he must be at least twelve winters old." He nudged Reim. "Right, boy?"

Reim nodded quickly, but immediately knew that he had done something dumb, because Karl kicked him in the shin, sending a sharp pain jogging through his whole body. The farmer hummed. "Oh no, you have not got a buyer in me, friend. I have to find a powerful workhorse, not just some sucking calf."

He walked over to a tall, light-haired boy who was standing beside a farmer from the corn district, and started transactions. "This is much better merchandise," he called over to his friend.

The light-haired boy cried. He hugged the old woman. But then he was forced to follow his new owner. "May the gods in Valhalla protect you," the woman called after him.

Reim glanced quickly at Karl. He was in a temper now, and Reim knew exactly what he was thinking. There weren't many buyers at this market. His friend had probably been right. The boy was both pale and weak, and his ribs stuck out right through his clothes.

"How much do you want for the little boy?"

Reim jumped. He knew that voice. A burly man in a brown sheepskin, hooded cape stood before him. Reim nearly broke out in a shout of happiness when he realized who it was. But the man winked hard at him, and Reim fixed his eyes on the ground, pretending not to care.

"One piece of burnt silver. He will grow to be big and strong with time."

"One piece of silver!" The hooded stranger nearly spit the words into Karl's face. "I would not give you more than a farthing for that skinny carcass. He might not even live through the year. I want a slave that can do some threshing for me this winter, and I will not be needing him any longer than spring. Don't try to trick silver out of me! Here is a farthing. If you do not take it now, you will not get him sold later!"

Karl shook his head. This was indeed a bad day. But he took the man's hand. The transaction was in order.

When they had reached the tall trees at the edge of the market place, Reim could not control himself any longer. He shrieked in relief and delight. He would have loved to thrown himself around Farmer Brede's neck, but he did not dare. He was Brede's slave now.

Brede laughed and pulled his hands through his grey tufts of hair. "That was the last coin I had. I would say that it was piracy! But we have little time to celebrate now. Our ship is ready for sailing. We have to get away from this place."

A noise made them stop and look back. "What in the world is happening down at the market place?" he wondered. "I am sure that I heard the bark of a person we both know well."

Reim peeked through the leaves. A chieftain from northern Norway pulled and dragged one of the slaves with him. "I paid two good pieces of silver for you, you beast," he hissed. "And it looks like those legs of yours are solid enough to carry you. So get going!"

The slave shouted. Swearing and cursing, he howled, "I am Earl Hakon's most trusted man. Don't you dare lay a hand on me!"

"I dare," the chieftain answered, giving the slave a blow across the back with his whip. "And you had better learn to watch your tongue, goatsbeard, or I am afraid that your life may end quite tragically!"

I guess that when the goddesses of fortune smile down on one, they turn their backs on another, Reim thought quietly to himself. But whether the saints or the gods preside here on this earth, life sure is strange.

"What did I say about dragging children with us on such a dangerous mission," Digralde growled when he saw Reim. Thus far everything had gone just as Digralde had hoped. Mistress Bergliot had welcomed her relatives graciously, and Farmer Brede was glad to have mighty Digralde with him during the first years in a new land. The only thing that had gone wrong was that this little Irish madcap had disappeared during the night. As a last chance, Farmer Brede had suggested taking a look at the market for this runaway colt, as he had called him. Vidur smirked and jabbed Reim in the side. "You have a tendency to always do things your own way!"

Una hugged Reim so that he nearly disappeared in her wide embrace. But Tir was furious, her eyes ablaze. "You fool!" she hissed. "If you had come just one day later, we would have been far out at sea already. How could you be so stupid!"

Reim flushed, but he could not help but smile. No one could get as angry as his sister. She would show her fists and hiss like a cat. Then she pulled her claws in again quickly. "And look at you, you are freezing," she said, as she threw her tattered cloak over his shoulders.

They made a strange group, these people gathered under Farmer Brede's roof. The sturdy men sitting on the long bench, in their brown sheepskin jackets, with well-cut hair and trimmed beards, were all farmers from the district. The women had kerchiefs over their hair and wore long woollen smocks, as was their custom. The smaller children sat on their laps, as the older children pulled at their mother's skirts persistently. Some half-grown boys and girls ran through the room teasing each other. In the middle of this flock sat the slaves, with their unkempt hair and beards, and their clothes in rags. They tried to keep a bit to themselves. Slaves were used to sitting quietly while free men talked.

Altogether, there were four ships ready to set sail. Mistress Aud owned one ship. She was a widow with four sons and had long since decided to head west to find new land. She had sacrificed to the gods and found out that this was a good year to make the trip. But then she had received word that her oldest son was dead, killed during a battle in Frankland. She had had to postpone her trip from full moon to full moon, so she could complete a grave mound for her dead son in the land where her ancestors had rested since time immemorial.

It was late in the year, but they had to leave. The farmers had prepared for this voyage the whole summer through. All of the trunks were packed with their everyday clothing and bedding. They had leather sacks filled with grain and large barrels with salted and fresh foods. It had taken several days to butcher all of the animals. "It has been a bit of a bustle, but now everything is ready for sailing, is that not right, my husband?"

Farmer Brede scratched his beard. He paced over to the door opening and looked out across the bay. The sea was dark grey, the same colour as the sky. Far, far out he caught a glimpse of white caps.

"I am afraid that this is not good weather to start out in," he said shortly.

"But the wind is from the mainland," Farmer Torolv protested. "If we are lucky, we can reach Iceland after only a few days with this wind."

Brede did not answer. He stood looking out over the bay, deep in thought. A third farmer, sitting in a corner, stood up.

"I think Torolv is right. We have to leave now, and we dare leave now. I do not know what you are afraid of, Brede. We have a war going on here. It looks like the fighting between the earl's men and the Illuges' will continue for a long time. And we cannot get around it, our farms are right in the line of fire. If we lose our lives on our farms or at sea, I really cannot see the difference. Personally though, I would prefer a wet grave to a hot one...ha, ha, ha."

Bergliot nodded decisively. "Then it is decided," she said. "The goddesses of fortune have protected us thus far. We cannot expect our luck to hold out forever. Start carrying the trunks and boxes down to the strand during the night. We will bring the animals on board last."

Bergliot handed Reim a goblet with a herbal drink. "If what you tell is true—that you have lay in ice water half the night—then you had better drink this up." Reim wrinkled his nose, but knew by the firm look on the mistress' face that he had no choice. He downed the scalding hot drink.

"I think we had better let our runaway slave sleep here in the house tonight," Brede said. "But the other slaves can hide out in the pig pen. I do not know of any other solution. There are too many warriors out hunting down runaway slaves this night."

Hunting down slaves, hunting down slaves... the words flew around and around in Reim's heavy head. He sank down on the pallet, just as his body started swaying, rocking him into dreamland. And suddenly he seemed to float high, high up in the sky, over the fields and forests, back to the place he had just left....

The first pale sun beams had just reached the sod roofs at the earl's farm. The farmyard was in confusion after the night's battle. Several men and two horses lay lifeless on the cold ground. Broken spears and arrows were spread throughout the yard, and a helmet with no master had rolled all the way down to the little creek, landing next to the slave quarters. Where the storage house had been, smoke rose from a pile of blackened logs, the ashes still glowing. Death and catastrophe filled the yard.

The earl's wife sat, pallid and exhausted, in the high seat, next to her son. There, she received word that twelve of the earl's men had fallen, and that three of them were most probably captured, among them

Orm Viking. She moaned, "Woe is me, to live this day. Never anything other than warring and feuds. Not long ago, my four small sons ran playing in this farmyard. Now, three of them are dead: two fell in viking raids in the west, and the oldest was cut down by the Illuges." She hid her face in her hands. Suddenly she rose, her eyes flaming. "Do not fail to take revenge for your oldest brother's death, Sigurd!"

She called to one of the warriors, "Fetch the slaves! It is high time to rid up in this battle field just outside of our door!" But the warrior returned shocked speechless. Slowly he stuttered, "The slaves have escaped. Only the old slaves and some of the half-witted young boys are left...."

"Where is Digralde?"

"He is gone, my mistress."

"And Una? Vidur?"

"They are gone too, my mistress."

"Then I expect that Reim has disappeared, too. And Tir," Sigurd said so softly that no one heard. "Just think, if I could go too...."

The mistress' face darkened. She could not get along without her slaves. They did all of the work on the farm; made the food, milked the animals, chopped the wood, ploughed the earth....

"Pack of bandits!" she shouted furiously. "Did they not receive food and clothing from the earl? Not one trustworthy slave to be found these days!"

She sat, sulking, until Sigtrygg Viking walked into the hall, announcing that he had good news. They had received word that the chieftains in the corn district, were on their way with several hundred warriors, all heavily armed. They had also heard a rumour that the King himself had given his word to help protect the young earl against further attacks from the neighbouring farms.

A shout of victory rose from the earl's men when they heard this. They all gathered in the hall. Sigtrygg Viking went forth with the news. They had come out of the attack fairly well, he reported. Some of the earl's men had fallen, it was true. But they had not managed to steal any of the many treasures, and the earl's seat was secure until Dovre fell. Why make such a bother about some runaway slaves? Next year they would sail out on new viking raids. They would return with new treasure and new slaves, with young, fresh blood in their veins. As long as they had their fast ships and their sharp swords....

The skald rose and praised the dead earl. He had been a brave warrior and exceedingly rich. May his own son, the young earl, be equally blessed, when he set out on his first hazardous viking mission this summer.

The men filled their goblets with mead and toasted victory. They continued the rest of the day. As the moonlight shone down through the smoke hole, they told exciting stories of their long excursions, and dreamed of the treasures that awaited them next year. They competed, trying to capture the young earl's attentions.

But Sigurd sat, silent and grave, in his high seat. His thoughts were elsewhere. It was as if they flew away on the golden strip of moonlight, higher and higher, over the rooftops of the farm.

His face finally brightened when a little buffoon entered the room and made his dog jump through a hoop he had stripped from a wooden barrel.

"Continue," he shouted in amusement, and laughed at the little, quick farm dog. And then he gave his first command as earl. "Give this man an arm ring of gold and make sure that his dog has a juicy bone for his dinner!"

As the skies brightened over the mountain ridge in the east, the four immigrant ships were already far out in the bay. Stygg mountain rose, green-blue and steep, on the starboard side. Light snow flurries whirled around the top.

"When will we get there?" the children pestered constantly.

Farmer Asbjørn stood at the helm. He knew this coastline as well as the seams in his breeches. "If the gods are with us, we will reach Iceland within ten to twelve days," he said. "But if the wind turns, it can take us a month or more. Many dangers lurk on the way. Vikings and pirates can ambush us. And if we get through this coastline area without grievous problems, a new and mightier foe awaits us—the great sea itself."

The children ducked beneath the railing and stared at the garden of islands passing beside them. Thousands of islets and holms were scattered throughout the surface of the grey water, some with trees, and others with steep cliffs and mountains. They anticipated hearing shouts from the top of the mountains at any moment, and they feared the rain of arrows that would accompany it. But the only shrieking they heard came from the sea gulls circling around the ship's mast. There were no foreign pirate ships to be seen, even though this was an area where thieves and vikings had harried the most.

As the ships crossed the outermost rocky reefs, they realized that the first serious obstacle on their trip had been overcome. Shouts of jubilation rose to the skies as the first sails were hoisted. The ship cut the waves with great force.

"And now we have the mighty sea," Asbjørn called from the helm. Waves sprayed across the ship's deck, and he was already soaking wet; wet right through his tightly woven russet jacket. "But at this speed we should reach Iceland quicker than any other landsmen before us!"

The ship rolled violently from side to side. The sea surrounding them was grey and the sky above them was grey. Asbjørn furrowed his eyebrows. He caught a glimpse of the sun covered by a dense haze, and it seemed to be getting darker by the minute. Soon they would not be able to distinguish the signs in the sky that they needed to keep the ship on course. It would be easy to drift off in wrong direction.

"May the god of the sea, Njord, be with us!" Brede shouted through the wind. He was clutching the ropes, holding himself upright, as the wind tore at his beard.

Tir and Reim and the other children crawled under the ship's tent. There, Una and Bergliot and the other women had placed a few chips of wood in an iron pot and lit a fire. They hung pieces of meat over the glowing ashes.

"Help yourselves now, children," Bergliot smiled. "But chew the meat slowly. We do not know how long we will have to be at sea."

Tir did not feel like eating. It was as if the waves were sloshing back and forth inside her stomach. She buried her head in the warm wool of one of the sheep and lay down moaning and groaning. It was not easy to lay still. Buckets and trunks, pots and pans all flew around the floor of the tent. Reim decided to teach the children the letters that he had learned to draw at the monastery school. But he soon had to give up. The ship tilted, so that his knife slipped as he carved his letters on a piece of wood and he made a deep cut on the flat of his thumb, which bleed profusely.

"Children should not be allowed to play with sharp iron," Brede said. He tore up some rags and bound the sore.

Digralde sat, as steady as if he was planted on Mother Earth, in the furthest corner of the tent. There, he talked of how wonderful everything was going to be in the new land. They should be able to build a house before the autumn storms set in with full force. He would use his full strength, and it would show in the results.

Una was looking forward to seeing her little daughter again. And Aud talked about the farm that she would build for herself and her sons.

Towards evening, Vidur, who was standing at the helm, shouted, "Clear skies ahead!"

Reim crawled out of the tent onto the deck. Oh! What a wind! The waves broke, crashing against the side of the ship. The deep sea gurgled and gurgled so frightfully. But overhead, the sky was studded with sparkling stars.

A little further away, stood Tir.

He was startled to see that she resembled their mother as she stood by the railing. She had grown this past summer, and was not just a little girl any longer, it seemed.

When she noticed him, she walked towards him on unsteady legs, her hair blowing out behind her like a sail. "Booooooo, here comes the sea monster!"

"Quiet! One does not joke about such things out here at sea," Reim shuddered. But then he laughed, "I have never heard of a seasick sea monster either, one that just lies holding it's stomach all day long!"

She pulled his coarse hair. "You are a terrible tease, Reim!"

"Reim," he pouted. "Forget that name...."

"Forget your slave name? Never! We are just as much slaves now! We have just changed our masters!"

He whispered in her ear, "But our chances for freedom are much greater now. We can hope, and maybe when we get to Iceland...."

She laughed a bit uncertainly. "Oh Patric...!" His name felt strange to her tongue.

"Yes, Sunniva."

"Do you see what I see?"

He tilted his head back and stared into the twinkling heavens. And then he knew what she meant. There, right in the middle of the whole system of stars, he saw the little star wagon they used as a guide when they had wandered a bit too far from home. It used to throw its light right down onto the roof of their farm house in Ireland. Now it glittered and blinked restlessly in the windy night. A sign to them, from a place far, far away.

"Strange that we did not notice that, the whole time we were slaves in Norway!"

"Yes, it is strange."

"Sunniva, do you think that sometime we may be...."

He did not finish his sentence. He knew that she would just shake her head and say the same thing as Grandmother Gaelion would have said: "Why, you little pirate! No one knows his own destiny...."